WARRIOR GIRL

WARRIOR GIRL

CARMEN TAFOLLA

 Nancy Paulsen Books

NANCY PAULSEN BOOKS
An imprint of Penguin Random House LLC, New York

First published in the United States of America by Nancy Paulsen Books,
an imprint of Penguin Random House LLC, 2023

Copyright © 2023 by Carmen Tafolla

Nancy Paulsen Books & colophon are trademarks of Penguin Random House LLC.
The Penguin colophon is a registered trademark of Penguin Books Limited.

Visit us online at PenguinRandomHouse.com.

Library of Congress Cataloging-in-Publication Data
Names: Tafolla, Carmen, 1951– author.
Title: Warrior girl / Carmen Tafolla.
Description: New York: Nancy Paulsen Books, 2023. | Summary: "A novel in verse about the joys
and struggles of a Chicana girl who is a warrior for her name, her history, and her right to choose
what she celebrates in life"—Provided by publisher.
Identifiers: LCCN 2023007857 | ISBN 9780593354711 (hardcover) | ISBN 9780593354728 (ebook)
Subjects: CYAC: Novels in verse. | Self-esteem—Fiction. | Schools—Fiction. | Family life—Fiction. |
Mexican Americans—Fiction. | LCGFT: Novels in verse.
Classification: LCC PZ7.5.T24 War 2023 | DDC [Fic]—dc23
LC record available at https://lccn.loc.gov/2023007857

Printed in the United States of America

ISBN 9780593354711

1st Printing

LSCH

Edited by Nancy Paulsen
Design by Marikka Tamura
Text set in Albertina MT Pro

To all the ancestral peoples of this City of Compassion,
who left us the values of
strength, celebration, and peaceful compassion
for those who are different from us,
and to all the young guerreras and guerreros who will shape
the world we live in tomorrow.

LIFE SLAPPED HER HARD HAND

Felt like Life had slapped her hard hand
over my mouth
and tried to shut me up,
tried to keep me
from being me,
keep me from even my song,
even my name.
Yes, she tried to shut me up,
and for a little while,
she did.

HOW I GOT MY NAME

So when I was born, my mom said, *Ay, qué preciosa.*
I want to name her Celina. But my dad said,
I want to name her after your mom, Teresa.
And Mom nodded (kind of) and said,
We'll name her Celina Teresa,
and we can call her Tere around the house
so Gramma can know how much we love her.
And they did.

And everything was good with my name except for one thing:
My dad's last name is Guerrero
and my mom's is Amaya,
and the nurse got confused when she saw
"all those names"
(Celina Teresa Guerrero Amaya.
I don't think four is too many names,
but I guess the nurse did),
so she wrote down Guerrera
with an A at the end of the name instead of an O.
And dropped the Amaya completely.

No one noticed right away 'cause they were
too busy oohing and aahing over me.
Then the birth certificate came in the mail,
and they noticed it and Dad just laughed.
He said, *Well . . .* Guerrera *means a "WOMAN warrior."*

I bet she'll be brave and strong and fight for justicia.
And then he said, *We could get it fixed later . . .*
Maybe.
And Mom repeated, *Maybe . . .*

Then, the very next month,
they deported my dad back to Mexico
for not having the right papers.

Funny how papers can be so right and so wrong
and can even mean more than people
in some folks' eyes.

WHAT MATTERS

Luckily, my dad returned to us pretty soon
because there's no way he was gonna leave
my mom alone to raise their beautiful baby girl (me).
Mama said to get back, Dad had to work to raise money
and borrow some from his cousin too.
He had to swim across a river at night
and then cross a desert with no water
and then walk through a field of snakes,
but he came back.
And he kept working here to pay for the rent
and for the food and the diapers.
He kept trying to get his papers,
but something else always had to be paid first,
like taking me to get my shots
or getting the motor fixed on the car
or learning enough English to do his taxes
or working to help Mama pay for her nurse's aide schooling.
But nothing was going to stop him
from being there for me
and being the best dad,
and that's what really
matters.

GRAMMA SAID I WAS WONDERFUL

Life is so much fun,
so rica with adventure and dreams
when you're little and at home
with people who love you and look at you with eyes full of
hope.

That's what my grandma did.
She looked at me
(even when I was bad and snuck an extra pan de polvo
off the plate before the party)
and laughed and said,
¡Qué sinvergüenza esta muchacha!
Even though her words said I was rascally,
that's not what her eyes said.
I saw her eyes.
They said I was
Wonderful.

COULDN'T WAIT

I couldn't wait for the first day of first grade.
I was big. I was cool.
I was ready to go
and show la teacher that I was
smart and pretty and wonderful . . .
I even put TWO bows in my hair
so that I'd look "bien purty."

I thought first grade was going to be
better than Christmas!
But instead of getting things,
we'd be learning things.
And I especially wanted to show the teacher
that I already knew how to write my name
in BIG letters, like a BIG girl:
TERE.
Tere, the name of my grandmother.
And my grandmother's grandmother.
And my grandmother's grandmother's
grandmother.

I remember that day so clearly,
remember bursting with excitement.
But sometimes things
don't turn out the way you
hope.

FIRST-GRADE TERE TELLS HER STORY

My teacher was so pretty.
A big, tall lady with blond hair.

But our first conversation went like this:

Hi. I'm Miss Jones.

Hi. I Tere.

Awww . . . Terry.

No, iss Tere.

No, it's pronounced Terry.

Iss . . . per-nounce . . . Tere.

No. Watch my mouth. Teh. Reee. See?

No, iss Teh-reh. Iss always been Tere.

Look. Make your mouth like this and pronounce it right.
Teh. REEEE! That's what your name is here,
and you will learn to say it right.

Pero RIGHT iss Tere, miss.

She lookin' at me so mean. And her eyebrows,
they like two standing-up lines of mad,
so I say, *Okay*,
because no importa,
it doesn't matter.
I in first grade, I smart, and I want teacher lady
to like me.

ERASED

When I color the Cinderella princess,
I make her look like my big cousin,
with long black hair down to there
and blue glitter above her eyes.
But teacher says, *Cinderella has blond hair.*
She takes away my picture,
says, *Do it over. Do it right.*
And I think, *No importa*
'cause maybe she doesn't understand.

Then we go to the cafeteria, and the food looks weird.
I'm hungry after lunch, but *no importa,*
doesn't matter.
In gym I get my own coach (like in the Olympics).
He lets the boys go first to show us how to run the races
(even though I run faster than Juanito and Chale).
When I yell, *¡Córrele, Juanito!*
Coach comes over to scold me,
says, *This is the U.S. Speak English!*
So I say, *Run, Johnny. Run!*
Coach still looks at me funny.
But I think, *No importa*
'cause gym is over.

We go back to the class and teacher says
she's gonna teach us how to write our names.

I show her my paper full of big proud letters that say
TERE.
She erases my name!
Says I got too many capitals
and not enough *R*'s.
Tells me, *Do it over. Do it RIGHT!*
But my paper looks so empty
and I feel like I just disappeared,
got erased, turned invisible.
And it hurts.

So I'm glad we have a game at the end of the day
so I can show la teacher how smart I am.
Teacher explains the game: *When I touch your head,*
jump up and say your name.

I jump up, say, *TERE,*
and she mumbles something 'bout
putting me in the slow class.

I don't WANT to be in the slow class,
to move slow and run slow and act slow.
But I don't say anything.
I go home and take off my two bows.
I have first grade again tomorrow, but . . .

No importa.
It doesn't matter.

MOVING

We had to move.
I don't remember why.
My dad got a new job
or the old job finished
or didn't pay enough to stay.
The new town wasn't any bigger than the old one,
but the people were meaner to us
and I felt a lot more lost,
especially in school.

The teacher there must've taken lessons
from the teacher in the old place,
because she, too, changed my name to Terry.
Guess none of them liked
names that sounded like Spanish.
So they took away my name.
I wonder what is left
that they CAN'T
take away.

CELEBRATING A CHUBASCO

We didn't live with Gramma back then,
but she'd always come to visit
and tell us stories to remind us who we were.
The house would fill with laughter,
and nothing—nothing ever—
could keep us from celebrating everything.

One day when she arrived,
the summer sky changed in a flash.

Chubasco!
When your sweltering hot boring day
turns dark as night and the wind
begins to blow like magic
and heavy clouds roll in to throw a big surprise party
as they throw down a confetti of icy hail.

Chubasco!
When thunder booms so big Gramma says it sounds
like a huge fiesta with someone banging hard on the drums.
But you and Dad watch it while sitting safely on the porch
and laugh and pretend to play drums
right along with the sound that beats down
from that cool wild drummer in the sky.

MY GRAMMA TERE TAUGHT ME

One of the things my gramma Tere taught me
was how to make a fiesta out of every day.
Every day she would whisper,
Today is a celebration! It's the feast of San Fulano de Tal!
And she would tell me the name of
the saint for that day
or the celebration for that day
or the reason we should be happy that day.

El Día del Mariachi! So we'd listen to mariachi music.
El Día del Chef! So we'd cook something special and exotic.
El Día de la Risa! So we'd spend the day joking and laughing.

Now I know why *Tere*
is just as strong a warrior name as
Guerrera.

Because when you're celebrating,
when you find a reason to be happy,
a reason to sing or dance or paint or play or laugh or write,
they haven't taken everything
away from you.

BECAUSE HE HAD NO PAPERS

Because he had no papers,
my dad could only get the temporary jobs.
The ones that didn't pay enough,
the ones where he had to work long hours,
the ones that disappeared from one day
to the next with no warning.
So we would move
and move
and move.
Sometimes he worked picking oranges.
Sometimes he worked building houses.
Sometimes he worked on chicken farms.
Sometimes he worked pouring concrete sidewalks.
But each night he came back to ask me, *How was school?*
And if I was already asleep, he'd just kiss me on the head.

ABOUT TEXAS AND MEXICO

In fourth grade, the teacher said
we were going to learn about Texas and Mexico.
We'd never talked about Mexico in school before, so
I was excited. I blurted out, *My dad is from Mexico,*
and my mom's family is from Texas since long ago,
when Texas WAS Mexico!
But they ignored me.

Our teacher showed us pictures of "The Heroes of the Alamo."
Then she showed us pictures of the Mexican soldiers,
every single one brown-skinned and with moustaches,
crawling over the walls of the Alamo
and stabbing the every-single-one-white Texans with bayonets.
The Mexicans were sneering. The Texans were bleeding.
I said, *That's just a painting. Paintings can be made up.*
Are there any photographs from someone who was there,
to show what really happened?
Teacher ignored me and a couple of kids pointed at me
and laughed.

Later, I looked Alamo up
and found out there were Mexican Texans,
and Black Texans, too, who were
fighting alongside those "Heroes of the Alamo."
They weren't in the paintings the teacher showed us.
And after the Battle of the Alamo,

some of them left the new Texas for Mexico,
because in Mexico slavery was against the law.
But in the U.S. it was legal and
those "heroes" were fighting to the death
to make slavery THEIR law
in their new nation.

DREAMS

That night, my head was swimming.
Maybe drowning from what I'd learned.
I lay down, and Mama said, *Sweet dreams, m'ijita.*
But I couldn't dream.
And I couldn't sleep.
When Dad came home, I heard him at my bedroom door,
but I didn't say anything.
He kissed my forehead, and I could feel his caring
even through my closed eyes.
Caring, even after so many long hours of work
fueled only by his dreams.
He dreams of being a part of this country—
a country he's chosen to work for, build, and defend.
And my mom dreams of finishing her training
as a nurse's aide, and someday being a nurse.
And me? What did I dream that night?
I dreamed of battles in textbooks, of ugly laws,
and of ugly walls that I hoped would crumble.
I dreamed you couldn't tell what color the soldiers were,
or which side they were on, or what they were fighting for.
That maybe, instead of fighting, they were learning
how to work and live together.

THEY WILL NOT SILENCE ME

So most of my time in school
I learned to keep quiet,
'cause when I spoke up, I got in trouble.
Then, finally, last year I got a teacher
who was so cool he told us WE were cool!
He told us our voices mattered.
Don't let them silence you, he said.
He told us our families' stories
were part of history too.
He said we could write our history in a book
and put it in a library for all to see.
He told us we came from a long line
of strong people with powerful stories.
I felt like singing out!

But then we moved again.
I left behind that school, that home, that town.
But I took something with me.
Something singing deep inside me
in a voice that won't be stopped,
No matter what, they will not silence me.
They will not take my story or my joy
away from me.

ADDING AND SUBTRACTING

I didn't want to move again.
I didn't want to lose our little home
with the orange tree in the backyard.
Or the tiny town we lived in, with its big sky
and nighttimes full of birdsong.
But we had to. Dad's job, like before, was temporary.
And now it's okay,
because we live with Gramma.
In a friendlier city.
In a home full of plants and trees and pictures.
And all the love and fun and celebration
she brought with her every time she visited
is ours every day!
Plus, we get to see my tía more,
and my supercute five-year-old cousin, Jade,
and we get together for Sunday dinners.

In math I learned that when you lose a negative,
that's a positive.

And guess what?
It's true.

MY SHIELD

I come from a long line of people Who Know How
to keep their courage up and their love strong
and their kindness always growing,
Who Know How to keep their Birthday-Party Smiles
no matter if folks are giving them Trash-Day Dirty Looks.

I come from a long line of
rock-solid moms, dawn-braving dads,
and grammas who light candles of hope
that'll burn for a lifetime.
Grammas who teach you How To Build A Shield.

I built my shield to keep ugly things out.
I built my shield to let lots of love in.
I built my shield to protect me from
name-callers, tongue-sticker-outers,
dirty looks, dirty tricks.

I built my shield to welcome in
big dreams, warm smiles,
new friends, new hope.

I built my shield from love.
From the blessings an old woman gave me
when I was still too tiny to talk.
From glances honeyed with
Qué chula, qué maravillosa, qué wonderful.

And now my shield is unbreakable.
Able to protect me.
Or a friend.
Or even a whole pueblo.

AND I WILL DECIDE

When I was little
and I was Tere,
they made me keep silent.
They made me give up my name.
But now I'm about to start middle school,
and I have decided that this year *I* will decide
what I want to be called.
And I will decide which two *electives* I take.
Maybe it will be band or choir.
Maybe it will be PE with volleyball or PE with dance.
Maybe it will be auto shop! Or Spanish! Or Mandarin Chinese!
And I *will* make friends.
And I won't be scared (too much).
Because I will remember that Gramma showed me
How
To Build A Shield.

CELINA

The first day of school is a clean page,
and that clean page starts in two days.
A chance to start new, to create new worlds,
to become who you want to be.

I want to be Celina,
Celina Teresa.
And my friends can call me Celi.
(And Gramma, of course, will always call me Tere
'cause that's part of me too.)

I don't want to lose Tere,
but Celina is a chance to be
a brand-new, grown-up me.
A brand-new me
who will NEVER be
forced to shut up
who she is.

DEPORTATION IS AN UGLY WORD

Deportation sounds like *operation*
sounds like *amputation*
sounds like *dehydration*
sounds like *discrimination.*

I know a lot of words,
but *deportation* is maybe the ugliest.
Especially since last night,
when my dad got picked up
by some officers with guns
and taken to who knows where.
Again.

Gramma says, *Don't worry.*
Your papacito belongs right here with you,
and this is where he'll come back to.
Love is stronger than Borders.
Patience is stronger than Hate.

Mama is crying in the other room,
but when she comes out,
she tries to put on a smile for us
and I put on a sorta smile for her
and Gramma hugs both of us and says,
Just wait. In just a few months, he'll be back.
Diosito nos ayudará.

When I lay my clothes out
for school tomorrow,
I try to remember how excited
and happy I was
just a few hours ago
when I thought nothing
could hurt me.

SOUNDS EASIER

My sighs are so loud when I get home from school
that Mama can probably see right through them.
See how alone I feel.
See the cold faces of those kids in the cafeteria,
their sneers and glares reflected on my face.
I try to hide it,
but she can see my
upside-down smile.

So when Mama says,
I think Papita Frita needs a walk,
I just wanna hug her, I don't know why.
So I hug Mama tight, grab the leash,
and take my tiny, funny dog
out for a walk.

And,
just like going to the school cafeteria,
it sounds easier
than it turns out to be . . .

LECTURE TO MY SMALL DOG

Oh, Papita Frita!
Why do you insist on giving me
so much trouble every time I walk you?
Do you think that you're ten feet tall?
That I'm some cross between
a mammoth and a bear?
No, I'm only twelve years old!
And you don't even reach my knee!
So why must you bark like
a rabid wrestler ready for a fight
every time we pass a big, sharp-toothed dog
the size of a small elephant,
walking oh so well-behaved
on their owner's leash, with not even a growl
from their trunk of a throat
(which looks capable of swallowing
BOTH of us without a blink)?
You charge out to the end of the leash,
all while my heart beats wildly in fear you will be
eaten up in one swallow, and me in two.

Not a good idea, dog.
Not a good idea at all!

AND GET SOME TORTILLAS ON YOUR WAY HOME! MAMA SAID

So I was still feeling pretty down.
Alone-Down, Worried-Down, Missing-Dad-Down,
Don't-Know-Anyone-at-the-New-School-Down,
and Small-Feisty-Out-of-Control-Dog-Tempting-More-Trouble-
Down.

I wasn't mad.
I *never* get mad.
I just get down.
And my stomach hurt in that funny way
like I'm halfway between scared and worried.

Then I remember Mama wanted me to go
to the tortillería where the nice old lady always calls me *M'ija*.
(Either that or *Chula*.)
So I go in to buy a package of corn tortillas,
and the smell of cookies and pan dulce baking
makes me feel so warm inside,
and Señora Loera says, *Hasta la próxima, M'ija.*
Good to see you!

When I leave the store,
my stomach isn't hurting anymore.
When I get home, I open the white paper bag,
and right on top of the plastic bag of fresh tortillas

is a perfect pink cookie with bright pink frosting.
Just for me!

My dad always told me that was called *un pilón*.
That surprise, that magical something extra,
something you didn't pay for or expect,
but someone gave it to you just for being you.

And in my mind, I thank Señora Loera
for being just as sweet
as this pilón.

LIKE I'M TALKING TO SOMEONE

Writing comforts me because
sometimes when I write
I feel like I'm talking to someone.
I write lots because after supper
Mama goes off to work at the health clinic
and Gramma goes off to sleep, so I'm alone.
Not even a brother or sister to talk to.
Will I always be alone?
With just a piece of paper
to tell my troubles to?
Gramma and Mama care a lot,
but I don't want to worry them.
Don't want to see my pain made bigger on their faces,
like that pena was under a magnifying glass
but projected huge on top of their hearts.
Daddy I could have talked to maybe,
but he's not here. Again.
Like that time long ago when he was taken away
just weeks after I was born. But NOW.
Right as I'm starting middle school!
And for what?
Taken away for not having the money
to BUY his citizenship like so many others do.
He's lived here thirteen years.
Worked here. Followed the law.
Paid taxes. Fixed our streets.
Picked the food they sell at the store.

Served at restaurants where fancy people eat.
Paid the bills. Taught me to be honest
and to be kind to everyone.
But still the lack of those flimsy little papers
means that anytime they want,
they can send him back to Mexico,
where he'll have to work months
to make enough money to travel back home to us.
The lack of papers means that every day
we have to worry that they might pick him up,
like stealing a fruit off a tree that's not *their* tree,
a tree that's *my* tree.

NIGHT CONVERSATIONS

Can't sleep again, so I do what Dad and I
used to do when we were restless.
I go out on the porch and stare at the sky
and listen to the night.
The trees wave very gently at me
and rustle their leaves at me like a lullaby,
and it calms me just right.

I look at the moon and know my dad is looking at it too.
I feel the wind and know my dad is feeling it too.
I talk to Papita Frita, whose big eyes always listen well,
and sometimes to my gato, Dulce, who just purrs
and cuddles close.
But still,
it would be nice to speak to someone who speaks
English or Spanish
or any human language
back to me.

AN EMPTY CHAIR

She was in the corner of the cafeteria
with no one talking to her.
But there was an empty chair right beside her
and she looked friendly enough
(like she wouldn't bite).
So I sat down next to her.
Hoping Not to be treated superbad.
Hoping Not to be laughed at.
And I smiled.
And she smiled.
And we started to talk.
And now I have
a new friend.

I, La Shorty, La Flaca, La Nobody-Likes-Her,
La Wears-the-Hand-Me-Downs-from-Goodwill,
La Always-Looking-for-Somewhere-to-Sit-in-the-Cafeteria,
have a friend. A Good Friend!
And her name is La Liz.

And now not only do I feel like I'm taller
and smarter and not alone,
but I also feel stronger, like
Celina Guerrera, aka Wonder Woman!
(Did you know that Wonder Woman is a Latina?
My gramma told me so.)

I feel more ME!
And now no one can ever convince me
that ME
is NOT a cool thing to be.

LIZ

Liz Leos is her name,
and she's from Albuquerque, New Mexico.
And she has two younger brothers and a baby sister,
and her mom works as a hotel manager,
and her dad works at something else
I've never heard of.
And she loves baseball and history
and cheese enchiladas
and dreaming of adventures and the beach
(even though she's never been to the beach
'cause New Mexico doesn't have any beach at all).
She says her parents promised her
a big family trip to the beach
during Spring Break,
which is seven months away, and she's
so excited she's counting the days,
marking them off with
an X on the wall calendar.
I guess I'm lucky because we go to the beach
at least once a year since we've always lived
only a few hours away.
Liz is tall and dark, knows lots of facts,
and is good at history.
She's quiet, upbeat, and always stays calm—
even when I drop my tray at lunch
and everyone turns to stare,
she just smiles and shrugs like it's no big deal.

Funny how we're different
in so many ways,
but she never makes me feel bad
for being who I am.
Guess that's what good friends are like.

WHAT A FRIEND IS LIKE

Having a friend means
you don't have to eat alone in the cafeteria.
And when something
horrible or disappointing happens,
it's not so bad when you can tell your friend
and they're good at listening.

Today I told Liz about my dad.
About how it's not fair for them to take away
a person who works so hard
and is kind to everyone
and so important to me.
How I hate the thought of a human being needing
papeles
to be respected.
How paper shouldn't be an enemy.
It should be a friend, like it is to me
when I'm alone
and need someone to talk to,
and it always listens so well.

Liz said I had *a way with words,*
that I was good at *putting feelings into words,*
that I was *smart in so many ways.*
That I should be a writer.

A writer?
Can you imagine that!
And she was being HONEST!
So I didn't contradict her and just said
thank you.

I DON'T GET MAD

Liz said, *I'd be so mad! Aren't you angry*
at the people who took your dad away?
And I tell her, *No. I don't get angry.*
I don't like angry.
Angry people are the kind that blow up.
I don't blow up. Ever!
So I don't get angry.

Liz looked me straight in the eyes.
She didn't say anything,
but her eyes were asking a question.
So I whispered as my chest kinda crumpled,
I just get . . .
down.
And I don't like
being down.

And she answered, nice and calm and kind,
Always be who you WANT to be.

But somehow it sounded like she said,
It's okay if you're angry.
I don't mind if you let it out.
It's sometimes better being angry
than being
down.

HANGING OUT AT LIZ'S HOUSE . . .

Mama said I could go to Liz's house
after school! We hang out in her room,
which is full of cool posters of beaches.
She has tall bookshelves packed
with tons of good books.
We paint our nails lots of colors, and
when we go to the kitchen for a snack,
her dad applauds like we are artists!
He says our nails look as beautiful and colorful
as a sarape blanket, and he gives her a hug.
The way my dad used to hug me all the time
when he was around.

Later we joke around and play video games.
And most important, we talk
about the way we wish the world would be.
I'm not even scared to tell Liz my gramma's stories:
My gramma says she and her friends got called names
and kicked out of swimming pools and restaurants
just for being Mexican.
But she was smart—she poured her anger into work,
kneading the masa hard for the tamales
that she and her mom sold till they had enough money
to buy the house Gramma still lives in.

Liz says, *Celi, you come from a long line of strong people.*
And—*I can't wait to meet your gramma!*

I tell Liz how my gramma is really fun to be with too.
How she turns every day into a holiday because
celebrating what you love gives you strength and energy.

Liz smiles and says, *I'll remember that.*
'Cause with two younger brothers and a baby sister,
I NEED more energy!
We need more holidays, too, to keep us strong,
so you and me are gonna start celebrating LOTS!

ADD UP THE TOTALS!

At first it's fun having six different teachers
in middle school,
but now every single one of them
wants to give homework.
Can they DO that?

An hour here
an hour there.
Just twenty minutes, they say here,
and *Just thirty minutes* there.
I wish they'd talk to each other
and add up the totals each night.
And when they say twenty minutes?
I wish they'd not count
how long it takes *them* to do it,
but how long it takes
me.

THE DEAL

We're trudging home after school, melting in the heat,
and I complain to Liz,
Middle school's messing with me, Liz!
Or maybe the mess is me. Way too much to remember.
Which class is third period, and which is fourth?
Which building is fifth period, or was it sixth?

Yeah, she agrees. *And how long your English paper's*
s'posed to be? Or was that the history paper?

YEAH! Too much to remember. But hey,
if I forget stuff, will you remind me?

Only if you'll help remind ME!
I forget stuff, too, you know, Celi?

Okay, and maybe that way each one of us
only has to remember half.

Deal.

Yeah, COOL deal!

KNOWING I HAVE SOMEONE I CAN TELL

I didn't tell Liz about the kids that looked at me funny today
when I was lost in the halls,
and who laughed at my beat-up shoes.
But I know I COULD tell her.
Maybe tomorrow.

And maybe I'll also tell her how those same three kids
made a face on the first day of school
when I tried to sit at their lunch table,
how they turned up their noses
like they were smelling rotten eggs,
and snickered when I left.

And while remembering this makes
my stomach feel like tangled knots,
at least now I have someone
who really hears me.
And somehow, those three kids' snickers
don't matter so much anymore.

THE LOSER

On the way to school I must've dropped my homework.
Then I lost my favorite hair tie right before PE
and my hair got all sticky and hot on my neck.
And then, when our English teacher asked us
to write down an idea for a poem,
I lost my thought and couldn't write down anything at all.
Sometimes I feel like such a loser! I tell Liz.
I know you say I have a way with words, but right now
I don't feel like I have a way with ANYTHING!
I lose everything! And I'm sick of losing things!

You're not a loser, Celi.
You're just tired of losing BIG STUFF.
Big things that are way more important
than homework or a hair tie!

I think of my father,
of the empty place at the table
and the empty place in my heart.
Liz is right.
And maybe I just find it easier to focus
on the SMALL things I've lost
rather than the BIG one.

TALKING WITH GRAMMA

Talking with Gramma can be
a splash of sunshine
in a dark, cold cave

can be a soothing voice,
calm and strong,
in the middle of a storm

can be a way of remembering
how delicious and wonderful
life sometimes is

can be a way to not feel
so all alone
when you don't have a dad around
to tell you the stories he used to tell
or do the fun things with you
you used to do
together.

GRANDPARENTS

(to ALL my ancestors)

I don't have my grampa Tacho anymore.
He died when I was four.
But Gramma says all my ancestors love me
and watch over me, even the ones I didn't meet.

When someone loves you, Gramma says,
that love never leaves your side,
no matter where your body or their body is.
The spirit of those we love is always there.

Gramma, you're so old and wise, I tell her,
and she laughs.

Hey! I'm just 68. Not THAT ancient!
In fact, I feel the same as when I was a child.
I suppose that inside yourself you're always you,
no matter how old you get.

So I ask,
What age do you FEEL?
And she says,
Seventeen. Definitely seventeen.

Then she tells me about her grandparents
and how when they were young,

of course it was *their* grandparents
who were the old ones.

And then one day, Celi Tere—surprise!
You will turn my age
and your grandchildren
will think YOU'RE ancient!

And I giggle. *Then they'll be wrong too!*
Just like I am now!

REWRITE

Ms. Yáñez, my English teacher, says
that a poem doesn't
have to come out "right"
the first time around.

That some poets rewrite
the same poem ten times
or a hundred times.

That there are tools poets can use
like a carpenter uses tools
or a painter uses colors
or a teacher uses examples.

And that getting personal
in a poem
isn't stupid.
It's beautiful.
Even when
it's about the pain you feel
every time you think about
your dad.

TOOLS

ALLITERATION is a lovely laugh
that lifts the spirit and soothes the soul,
so sweet its sound,
so soft its song.

And REPETITION's fun, fun, fun,
and then sometime
you'll use a RHYME,
or a . . .
SURPRISE!!!
ONOMATOPOEIA packs a pow,
creates a shush, a schloop,
disappears into a gulp, a glug, a gack!
LINE BREAKS add to the
suspense,
the power of each
statement
spoken slowly and
with care.

And TRANSLANGUAGING, that in-between space
where you're free to use ALL of your languages,
ALL of your styles,
adds emphasis and fun y, claro, ¡más sabor!
¡Qué cool!

And there's WRITER'S INTUITION…
which Ms. Yáñez says I have!
And HONESTY. *Just write your life!*

But METAPHOR's the queen,
la reina standing tall and powerful
in her land of crystal castles
built from words
while her royal choir sings stories,
gives emotion and connection
to her subjects, hungry for
these symbols of deep meaning.

These are the tools
Ms. Yáñez handed me,
which I now own
in my poet's toolbox.

MY VOICE

It doesn't matter if
I AM a great writer
or not
or if the poems I write
aren't perfect.
It only matters that they're in
MY voice.
And Ms. Yáñez says MY voice
is the most important thing I own.
She says it's
WHO I am
and
WHAT I feel
and
WHAT I want to say
and
HOW I want to say it.
So there!

And anyway,
I know *paper* is my friend.
It's only the *people*
who make paper stand
for what it
shouldn't
who
aren't.

TO WRITE OR NOT TO WRITE

I love writing so much that I'm scared,
I confess to Liz.

Scared of what? asks Liz.
Loving something usually makes your life better.

Scared that I'll run out of things to say.
Or that I'll write something I really feel
that is too dangerous to say.

What do you mean?
Are you scared of what you're feeling?

Maybe. You know, I'm realizing something.
I think sometimes I DO get mad.
Like when people say, Happy Labor Day!

But why? We get Monday off for Labor Day!
And my family's going to the zoo!

Well, it IS cool that we get Monday off.
But my mom doesn't.
And my dad never did either.
So if Labor Day is to celebrate ALL workers,
why do SOME people get the day off to relax
and SOME people have to work on that day,
and not be home celebrating with their families?

Liz is quiet, but then she says gently,
Want to come with us to the zoo?

And I answer, *No, thanks.*
I think I'll stay home and write.

YOU HAVE TO BE BRAVE

Ms. Yáñez says that it takes courage to write
but that it takes more courage to share that writing.
She says sharing can be reading it to a friend,
or reading it to an audience, like at a poetry reading
or a public event. Or sharing can be publishing
that writing in a book or newspaper.

Standing in front of an audience? Sounds so
frightening I blush when she just mentions it!

I imagine what I'd like to do with my writing,
and a tiny little whisper is scared to say out loud
that I would love to share it with people who
might understand what I'm saying.

Ms. Yáñez also says it takes courage to dream big.
That you have to be brave to become yourself.

I think that's why she's my favorite teacher. She
makes me feel that I can dream big. And someday
be brave enough to share my writing
and my dreams.

IT'S MY BEST FRIEND'S BIRTHDAY TOMORROW

Liz's birthday is tomorrow,
but I don't have anything to give her
and I don't have much money.
I look at some clearance stuff in the drugstore, but
I dunno . . . it's not really *her*.
I look through the old puppets on strings
my other gramma sent me from Mexico
'cause Liz always says those puppets are so cool!
Maybe . . . but I don't have money for a card, so . . .
I write a poem and wrap it up with a puppet.
I feel kinda bad but . . . Liz is like,
This is the best gift EVER!

Yeah, she thought the puppet on strings
that looked like Cantinflas was superfine.
But when she said *best gift EVER*,
she was talking about
my poem!

SATURDAY'S HISTORY LESSON

Liz's mom drops her at my house so we can study together
for the history test. It's way more fun studying together than alone,
but I sigh the minute we open our books.

Why do you hate history so much? Liz asks me. It's fascinating.
And I tell her about fourth grade and the first time I saw Mexicans
mentioned in my Texas history book and what they said about us.
Ouch! she says. What a terrible memory!

And it was WRONG history too! Here, I'll show you, I say
as I look up Alamo on the computer.
*You might not know this, Liz, but before Texas
was a state in the U.S., it was a state in Mexico,
but the new settlers there wanted to become independent,
and they wanted to fight Mexico's attempt to end slavery.*

Liz gasps. *The Texans were trying to KEEP slavery?*

Yes, here's a quote from Stephen F. Austin:
"Texas must be a slave country, circumstances
and unavoidable necessity compels it."
So now you know when our textbooks are calling the Alamo
"the Shrine of Texas Liberty,"
it sure wasn't liberty for the people they enslaved!

In total amazement, Liz starts swallowing up the articles I point out.

Wow, so the history gets retold in different ways by different people, and sometimes legends and heroes turn out to be not-so-heroic.

Yup, I say, but we'd better stop this and get back to studying OUR chapter (or Mr. Mason will find out how horrible I am at history).

You're not horrible, Celi. You're the best ALAMO historian I know!

FOUR WEEKS

Already, I've been in school four weeks
and am beginning to know lots of people.
But one kid in my math class is so quiet
that I wonder about him.
Some mornings I see an older kid,
maybe a relative,
waving. *Hasta luego, Chato!*
So I guess his name is Chato.
All I know is he seems sad.
And when he's in math, he looks worried.
Did he enter school late in the year?
I don't remember.
Does he work after school?
He looks so tired.
Does his family pick in the fields?
I worked one summer
with my family, picking strawberries
and then onions.
It was really tough work.
I don't usually think about it much.
But when I see HIM,
I do.

CHATO

No, Mees, ¡yo no sé NADA!
Chato blurts out, honest-hearted,
when Ms. Jackson says, *You know what X represents,*
and the whole math class busts out laughing.
He hides his worn tennis shoes
under the desk,
and his eyes turn low where we can't see
what they're thinking.
I hear his exasperated sighs
as he plods through the math problems,
and when he gives the teacher his paper,
his smile pleads with her to be kind.
She doesn't look up from her desk.
Doesn't see it.
Only I
see the hope that still grows
from the hands he is squeezing together,
head down
and shoulders
slumped.

SOMETIMES IT'S EASIER

Sometimes when you have one already,
it's easier to make another.
That's the way it is for making friends in the cafeteria.
Liz and I meet a girl named Cata,
and we all get along right away.

Then Liz tells her I'm a poet,
and I blush.

Cata begs me to let her see one of my poems,
and my notebook's open to the one about Chato.
I let her read it.
And she likes it! Then she says,
Maybe you could write a poem about me.

That night I try, and realize there's something
I love about how Cata speaks.
Something that is like poetry.
Something honest and strong.
Something unafraid.
The words start to flow
as easily as our friendship.

MY POEM ABOUT CATA (THAT SHE LOVES!)

So my name is Cata. COT. TAAHH.
But most people call me CAT-Uh.
Because some people think they
CAN'T
pronounce my name.

(Well, they CAN, but
they don't KNOW they can.)

They see C-A-T and
immediately,
they say Cat.
And then they see the A at the end,
and say Uh.
So they call me CAT-Uh.

I try to teach them,
but they close their minds.
Spanish pronunciation, to them, is like
on a different planet.
It's like they see ME as coming
from a different planet!

But I CELEBRATE
having two languages.

I LIKE the way life feels
when you can laugh in two languages
and share in two languages
and breathe in two languages.

Yup, my name is Cata.
COT-TAAAH!

CATA IS DIFFERENT

Liz is very quiet, always thinking, listening, kind.
And I can be quiet, too, sometimes, when I feel shy.
But Cata's not quiet OR shy at all.
She talks to everyone and speaks right out loud.
Why not? she says. *This is who I am.*
Always speaks straight from her heart.
Like a big surprise party—loud and fun.
Like a bright purple flower in a field of pale blue.
Like sparkly shooting fireworks in a night sky.
She's a people-lover and a flag-waver.
Ask her 'bout the Fourth of July and she's Red, White, and Blue.
Ask her 'bout the Dieciséis, and she's Red, White, and Green.
So which flag is your favorite? we ask.
All of them, she replies. *Every single flag that stands for human beings.*
And MOST days, I'm a blend. Red, White, and Turquoise!
Cata's so happy with her double languages and double cultures,
it sometimes makes you feel like you've got a double friend!

FRIENDS PAINT MY DAY HAPPY

I have TWO friends now that paint my day happy.
Twirl beautiful colors around school hours.
Decorate the air with laughter.
Even some evenings are splashed with their fun.
One will call, or the other will come over.
It's enough to almost make me forget all my worries.
Forget how empty things feel with Dad not there.

But these last few weeks, the homework's been heavy.
I go to bed yawning and wake up tired too.
Mom's on double shift, so me and Gramma do all the housework,
and no one's folks say they can come over to hang out.
By evening, we're all dragging—even Papita Frita,
who's so tired he doesn't yank me along on our walks.

Gramma strokes my tired head in the morning and says,
To everything there is a season. A time to work, and a time to play.
Don't worry, m'ijita. The time to play will come soon.
But every day, there's no time and too much homework!
And I'm missing my new friends, who keep me strong and cool.

DEAR MR. MASON

Dear Mr. Mason—
The history homework you assigned
makes me sad, makes me cry,
makes me ready to revolt.

First, that history textbook is so big and heavy
I have to squeeeeeeeeze
it into my backpack
and it almost breaks the zipper!

Second, I walk like thirteen blocks home,
carrying it like iron weights,
and I'm only twelve and
NOT a weight lifter!

Third, the chapter on the industrial revolution
was sooooo long it took me three hours to read!
But worst of all, I READ what it said!
In the industrial revolution, kids were forced to work
TEN hours a day or more,
and that was just plain wrong!

Mr. Mason, have you read this chapter?
I think you need to reread the line that says,
Child labor laws later made it illegal
to work children more than nine hours a day.

Mr. Mason, I worked hard SEVEN hours at school today,
plus THREE hours of YOUR homework,
and now I have to do math homework too.
That's more than ten hours.
And that's against the law!
Love, Your Student.

P.S. I'm really good at math.

YOU ACTUALLY SAID THAT TO HIM?

You actually said that to him? Liz asked me the next day
after I told her I'd complained to Mr. Mason.
Wow, that's cool.

Well, I didn't, like, say it to his FACE!
I just wrote it—impulsive-like—at the bottom of my homework.
That's not too rude, is it?

She's looking at my rough draft, which
I had scribbled in my purple notebook, of course.
It looks kind of like a poem, she says, tracing
the words softly, as if they were from a treasure map.

It also looks like . . . a protest. Something like a speech
that a leader would give to rally people when things aren't right.
Maybe THAT's why he said, "No homework tonight."
Celi, your pen has power.
The power of your voice.
You should write more.
It's cool when you Speak Up.

I'm not sure I really get everything she said,
but write more? Maybe.
Yeah.

EVERY PERSON HAS THEIR GIFT

It's October already, and I haven't even thought
about what to make for a Halloween costume.
Then it comes to me—this year I should be a calavera,
clanking my bones through streets full of skeletons.
I can wear it when I take my little cousin Jade trick-or-treating.
And then I can wear it again on the Day of the Dead!
But while my imagination is very good,
my skills at drawing are NOT.
I notice Chato scribbling away on his margins.
His sketches are great!
When I ask for advice on making the foot bones,
he beams. *I can paint it for you!*
And that very afternoon, he comes over to help
till we design a supercool costume.

Then I notice Chato's math book,
with a crumpled, over-erased homework sheet inside.
I smile and offer, *I can show you how to do these problems . . .*
And so I do.
It feels good to be sharing our skills with each other.
Gramma says, *Cada persona tiene su tesoro, su fuerza, su don.*
Every person has their treasure, their strength, their gift.

WHAT DO YOU MEAN COLUMBUS DAY?

Lots of people in the U.S. will still be calling this October holiday
"Columbus Day" 'cause that's when he came
and supposedly "discovered" America.

I ask Mr. Mason,
What kind of man goes around saying
HE discovered America?
I mean, we all know that Native Americans
were already living here for thousands of years.
And what made Columbus think he had the right
to claim this land belonged to HIS king?

Mr. Mason just looks at me, kind of surprised.
But the next day he comes back and tells the class,
Columbus was one of many people, of different nations,
who landed in the Americas in the centuries
after the Indigenous civilizations had developed there.
Indigenous peoples have lived on this continent
for well more than twenty thousand years,
and that's why many states and cities now call
this holiday "Indigenous Peoples' Day."

Then he blushes a little and mumbles,
I felt it important to correct my own mistakes
after a very intelligent student pointed out the biases
in my lecture yesterday.

And then he smiles at me, and says,
Maybe that student should write a poem about it
that we can use in teaching future classes.

And so I did!
And I might even read it out loud someday.
(Maybe I am getting braver.)

THE DISCOVERY

Gramma jokes, *When MY ancestors saw*
Columbus landing and kissing the ground,
he was SUPER lost! He thought he was in India!
So if anyone wants to talk about Columbus discovering America,
explain to them that he was LOST!
And America discovered HIM!

My gramma says her family comes from right here,
has been living here since before it was the U.S.,
or Mexico, or even San Antonio.
Her people called it Yanaguana.
Gramma says, *When the Europeans came,*
they changed our city's name. Changed OUR names.
Tried to change our language and religion too.

My gramma corrects anyone
who says the Indians disappeared.
'Cause we're not gone.
We're still right here.
Named García and Martínez, De León and Delgado,
Campos and Flores, Hernández and Sánchez.
We might speak Spanish. We might speak English.
But our blood is still the same.
We love this land. We love our culture.
We love sharing gifts with all who come.
Our generous cultures have given you so much:

Chips and salsa, ketchup and fries,
chewing gum, chocolate!
Two houses of Congress, hammocks to relax, and a zero for math.

Thanks to Gramma, I made a discovery—
the real history of America.
And lots about my own history too.

I DID IT! (AKA WHAT A WEEK!)

I finally get my Halloween costume all made
(with Chato's help).
And finish the notes on my history paper
(with Liz's encouragement).
Also finish helping Chato with math
and Cata with English
(when we weren't cracking up
laughing at all of Chato's jokes!).
And even finished cutting squares
for Gramma for a new quilt.
(She's making this one red, Dad's favorite color,
for when he gets home,
which has got to be any week now,
I'm sure!)

And now I'm finally free to help Gramma
put up the altar
to the dead.
But just REMEMBERING what Heather said
makes me upset.
Gramma says, *Who's Heather?*

Just a kid at school.

She must be important to you if her opinion matters.

It just makes me angry when she turns her nose up
at everything Mexican, as if it's not as good.

Well, what did she say?

She said Day of the Dead is "just Mexican Halloween."

Gramma says, *Well, how can she know unless you explain it to her?*

And so the next day, I do.

WE CELEBRATE OUR DEAD

No, Día de los Muertos is NOT "Mexican Halloween."
It's the Day of the Dead.
And the skeletons and candy skulls
are NOT meant to be scary!
They are meant to be happy!

Really? Why? Heather asks.

Because we love our family,
whether they're here or not.
And they're not scary,
'cause they love us too!
And they're still our family,
whether they're dead or not.
So this is a way to celebrate with them,
invite them to dinner,
and keep them always in our hearts.

No, it's not celebrated on Halloween.
It's the first two days of November.
And no, DON'T dress as a ghost
on Día de los Muertos. That's disrespectful!
And NO, not a vampire or zombie either!

Tell you what.
Just come to my house
and my gramma will show you our altar

and you can join us for our celebration,
and eat a candy skull, and
we'll paint our faces like happy skeletons, and—
What? You think that's So-o-o-o Coo-ool??
YESSSSS!!!

SURPRISES

Sometimes life surprises you.
Like I wasn't sure about inviting Heather over,
didn't know what would happen . . .
but she immediately fell in love with Gramma
and the whole idea of Día de los Muertos.
Then Heather told us how her grampa had died last year
and no one talked about him anymore.
And then she stared at our altar,
at all the pictures of family and friends who had died.
(Some were people who'd died even before I was born!)
And she asked, kind of timidly,
could she bring her grampa's picture here?
And Gramma said, *Yes, of course.*
We'd be happy to have him at our altar,
but you'll have to tell us what you loved about him
so we can love him and remember him too.
So now our altar includes a picture, an orange, and a baseball cap
for Grampa John Allen McIntosh.

Yup. Sometimes life surprises you.

SACRED AND GOOD

Gramma's making homemade flour tortillas,
and I can smell papa con huevo on the stove.
This usually makes me happy, but I must be looking sad
'cause Gramma asks, *What's bothering you, m'ijita?*

It's what I saw on TV last night, I tell her.
People shouting at the camera. Shouting about Mexicans.

They don't know better, m'ijita.
Some of them are just repeating things they've heard.
And just 'cause someone SAYS something
doesn't mean it's true.

But it's not just them, Gramma!
Even some kids at school repeat this stuff.
Talk about asylum seekers like they're criminals,
not people seeking freedom.
They say Mexicans try to come here for a free ride!
But we work so HARD, and I don't see ANY free rides!
And it's not just Mexicans seeking asylum. It's all wrong!

Gramma hands me the warm papa con huevo taco
and a cup of hot chocolate, and says,
Remember, just 'cause people say things
doesn't make them true. Remember:
Use your shield to keep ugly words away from you.

Then she puts her arm around my shoulders, makes
the blessing sign on my forehead again and again,
and tells me, *You are valuable. You are important.*
You come from cariño and courage and creativity.
You come from love.
Child of the universe, sacred and good.
Sacred. And good.

And finally
I feel strong.
Really strong
again.

GRAMMA DID WHAT?

I'm feeling pretty good as Gramma and I finish
off our breakfast tacos,
till Gramma lets out the longest sigh.
I had hoped things would be much better by now.
It's been fifty years since we had the
Chicano movement protest marches.

WE??? YOU *were part of the Chicano movement?!* I gasp.

Yeah, I was seventeen and a senior . . .
ready to celebrate our history and
reclaim our rights in this land of ours.
Ready to change the world.

WHAT??? *MY GRAMMA?*

Is a warrior too!

While I wrap my head around that, she continues,
. . . And we did change things—even changed
SOME *of the school rules, after which*
we were no longer paddled for speaking Spanish . . .

THEY PADDLED MY GRAMMA

What do you mean, you got paddled
in school for speaking Spanish?!
I ask Gramma indignantly.

Oh yes, back then we had teachers who'd
hit us with thick wood paddles—
once for every word we spoke in Spanish.

I winced. *So is THAT why you protested?*

Oh, there were so many reasons to protest—
the schools where we Mexican American kids went
didn't offer advanced classes since they didn't
expect us to go to college.
They'd force us to change our names to English names.
My brother Rafael had to call himself RALPH!
We were tired of it all!
Ready to call ourselves what WE wanted to be called.
To decide for ourselves what jobs WE would like
or if WE wanted to go to college.
We needed to be able to follow our dreams.
We had asked and asked, and they wouldn't listen.
So one day we all walked out.
And many parents joined us in the protest marches.
Some store owners and college professors did too.
Soon, a young Mexican American ran for state senate,
and we got all our parents to go out and VOTE!

He was elected, and he passed the new bill.
No longer would speaking Spanish on school grounds
be against state law!
And you know what? They heard us!
The very next year they started offering college-prep classes.
And there was NO MORE PADDLING!

DR. GRAMMA

I'm always in awe of my gramma, but now I'm even
more in awe!
You changed all THAT?

Oh, not alone, and it didn't all change at once.
But if you work together, convince others to help,
and have patience, there are no limits
to what can get done!
Even though I wasn't able to go to college,
I wanted it to be easier for others to go and achieve their dreams.

I was still stunned. *You wanted to go to college?*

Gramma sighed. *Yes. I was interested in medicine—*
dreamed of maybe being a nurse, or . . . a doctor.

Gramma, you doctor up everything!
You heal my feelings AND my thinking!
You're the reason this whole family
is healthy and strong.
Strong like guerreras,
like warriors.

INVISIBLE, OR WHY I FEEL THE NEED TO SPEAK OUT

My history textbook is bumming me out!
Making me feel like I'm INVISIBLE
because no one wants to talk about the Mexicans or
other Indigenous people unless it's to paint us as savages!
No one is talking about how developed OUR civilizations
were, with lots of science and inventions and math,
and even the principles of democracy
(according to Mr. Mason, who's been slipping me
important facts ever since I asked about Columbus Day).
Mexican Indian civilizations gave us anesthesia!
And invented rubber!
Why aren't THESE facts in our history book?
Ms. Yáñez said there's a word for that—
it's called *Eurocentrism*.
A bias that makes people think things don't count
or don't even start till white Europeans get there,
and that things from European origins
are automatically better.
She says we need more history books that are *inclusive*,
not biased, written from multiple points of view.
Books that make people more aware and open-minded
so they better understand each other
and maybe even forget
to hate.

ACTIVE IS

Ms. Yáñez, I'm tired of just SEEING
that things aren't fair.
I want to get out there
and do something to make it CHANGE!

Yes, Celi, a lot of activists feel that way.

Active Is?

No. Activists.

Activists? I ask. Isn't that something bad?

No, Celi. Activism is about ANY action people do
that's designed to bring about change.

So if I want there to be more history books that show that
Mexican Americans are
a great part of this country
and belong here,
that's activism?

It is if you DO something about it.

Like writing the textbook makers a letter?

Exactly. Or maybe getting a LOT of people
to write the textbook makers a letter.
And helping people find what
a solution would look like.

Ms. Yáñez, I gotta go!
I've got to round up ALL my friends.
We've got a lot of work to do!!!

MORE FAIR

Two days later, I'm sitting with Cata and Chato and Liz
in Ms. Yáñez's classroom at the end of the day.
Ms. Yáñez is nodding her head as we tell her our plans.

We want to have an assembly or something,
to celebrate all the cultures in our school and
to let folks KNOW there are ways to make things more fair
and to make change actually happen.
But HOW, Ms. Yáñez, and where? And who?

I can help you organize a night event with the school.
Someone might have to read some poems, Ms. Yáñez says, and
she looks at me.
I nod excitedly and offer, *Maybe I'll write skits too!*

Someone might have to sing a protest song, Ms. Yáñez continues,
and she looks at Cata.
Cata gives a thumbs-up.

A few people might have to give a speech to explain their history.
Ms. Yáñez looks at Liz.
Liz starts taking notes.

We might need displays and posters and stage art. Ms. Yáñez looks
at Chato. He rubs his hands together eagerly.

But it all can be done, she tells us. *It'll just take time and planning*
and a good program that makes people laugh and feel good
and learn.

We can do it! Cata says. *And invite our friends and families too.*
What should we call it? asks Liz.
Making Our World More Fair, I shout, and everyone nods.

You'll need a lot of time to prepare, to plan, to write.
I ask, *Would early April be a good time?* (I don't tell them
it's because I'm thinking Dad'll for sure be back long before THEN
and can inspire me as I write.)

Yes, April would be a beautiful time! Ms. Yáñez agrees.

GRACIASGIVING

(a dramatic monologue, written by ME,
for our Making Our World More Fair event)

A lotta people today don't know that the REAL first
Thanksgiving dinner between Indians and Europeans was in
1519, Mexico City, a hundred years before that Plymouth one.

So let me tell you that when Cortés, in Spanish armor,
and Moctezuma, in his crown of jade and green feathers,
sat down to the first Thanksgiving,
Cortés didn't even know how to use a finger bowl!

How do I know?
Because I was there! I'm Moctezuma.
Yup, the very one! (But you can just call me
Your Royal Majesty, Emperor of the Aztec Empire.)
I ordered a full banquet table for our visitors
and invited them to eat.
Cortés bit into the tamales—with the shucks still on them!
Then he tried to drink the salsa! I thought, *Gee,*
he's not very good at table etiquette, is he?
So I said to him, *Uh, Hernán?*
You seem to need a lesson in
Aztec food and culture!

Try this. It's called chocolate. We drink it hot.
Later, you guys will put it in candy bars.
But for me, I just HAVE to have it hot, with every meal.

Oh, don't worry about those bees—
we've developed a stingless bee here!
After dinner, we'll take a tour of the Agricultural Research Center
and you can learn all about that.
You like books? We can show you the emperor's library too.
Then the beautiful grand highways—
FIVE LANES, plus a waterway on each side.
And so clean. Littering's against the law.
Here, have some of this.
It's called chicli. (You'll call it gum a few languages from now.)
And—NO, NO, NO, don't swallow it!
Just chew it. And keep chewing! Yes.

Don't they teach you
ANYTHING on your continent?

THANKSGIVING HOLIDAY

Yay! the whole class shouts when the
final bell of the day rings and school's out for
Thanksgiving week break!

At lunch, Cata, Liz, and I had talked about our plans.
Y'all know I live with my great-aunt, Cata said, *and
we usually travel to Mexico during holidays to visit
her sisters in Guanajuato, where I'm always the only girl
and they always wanna buy me dresses.*
But I LIKE my old jeans and sloppy T-shirts!
Liz sighed. *I'll be babysitting my brothers
while Mom and Dad work most of the week.*
*And I can't have anyone over or be on the phone,
because they don't want me to get distracted
'cause my little brothers get into trouble really fast.*
I didn't say anything,
but they knew what was on my mind—
Thanksgiving without my dad.
I *really* thought he'd be back by now.

So I guess none of us were looking forward
to this Thanksgiving break.
As we walk out of school, Liz, Cata, and I all sigh,
and it sounds like a chorus on key, so we laugh.
Then, right outside the door, we find Chato
picking up full Fritos bags some kids had tossed away.

Stocking up, he whispers to me.
For the days we aren't in school and don't get free lunch.

The four of us walk slowly away from the school,
not wanting to leave one another,
and a feeling bubbles up from inside me like a fountain.
Just when I'm feeling so low I wanna scream . . .
I realize my friends will always be there for me
even when we're apart.

And it's like Cata reads my mind when
she laughs like a firecracker and says,
You know when any of us get crazy lonely
and think we're gonna burst,
let's think of each other and we won't feel alone.

THE ANNUAL WISHBONE WRESTLING MATCH!

As I trudge closer to my house, alone, I notice
Gramma's put pumpkins on the porch.
A brisk breeze rustles the leaves, and suddenly
all the Thanksgivings I've ever loved
come rushing back to me,
and one of my favorite parts—
the annual wishbone wrestling match!
Dad always pretends to be a big brawny lucha libre fighter
and sets up a table for us to arm wrestle,
acting like he's gonna annihilate me.
We put our arms on the table,
giggling so hard we can barely breathe
as we each grab an end of the wishbone.
Ready? he asks. Then, *¿Estás segura?*
Then he does a big dramatic countdown, like *diez, nueve, ocho,*
siete and a half, siete and a fourth, siete and un poquititito,
six and a half . . . And finally, when we hit one,
he pretends to be struggling to beat me with all his might
and cries out in pain, and usually I win.
But we all laugh so hard the whole family feels
like everybody won.

Then I hear the leaves rustling and neighbor dogs barking
and I open my eyes. To today, without him.

I sigh. And try to focus on how inviting
Gramma's pumpkins look.

WHO WINS

So Thanksgiving's here,
and I'm staring at the turkey.
As Mama carves it, she lays the strips of meat on a platter
and quietly sets the wishbone aside with a sigh.
When she notices I've seen, she tries to act happy
and says, *Ay, m'ija, you'll get to have a wish later on.*

And everybody gets quiet,
thinking the same thing,
remembering the same person
who isn't here.

Then Gramma says to Mama, softly,
M'ija, YOU get to have a wish too.

And later, when Mama and I both pull on that bone,
our eyes a little moist,
we both pull gently
and it doesn't matter who wins
because we both
have the same wish.

WHEREVER

The bad thing about having a long holiday
is that it gives you lots of time to think
and worry even more.
Where exactly is he?

Every other Thanksgiving of my life
he was here.
And I wonder
where he is now.

Do they have him in one of those cages
they've set up at the border
to lock up people who don't have the right papers?
Where people get sick and hungry
and no one cares?
Where there's no beds and no blankets?
And they can't call anybody
to let them know where they are?

That night when I get into bed
I only use one little corner of the blanket
as if I could save the rest of it
to keep him warm
wherever he is.

WHAT I WANT FOR CHRISTMAS

The world is bursting with holiday spirit,
tamales and Santa Claus and pictures of snow.
Mama smiles and asks me what I want for Christmas.
She tries to always look strong
and always be cheerful
and be like the star that shines out from the top
of our Christmas tree every year.
Steady and sparkling
and filled with kindness and joy.

But late at night, I see the starlight flicker and go dim
when she doesn't think I'm looking.
And her eyes are red from crying.
Like mine.

And then I think of little Jade,
cute and fun and funny and only five years old,
who NEVER gets to see her dad
except maybe once every year or two,
and who REALLY, REALLY wants the
Coolest Little Kid Toy of the Year—
a purple punch-button guitar.

So I ask Mom,
Do you think Tía will have enough money to buy it?

Mama sighs, as honest as always. *Your tía's thinking of*
taking a side job two nights a week if she can find a sitter.

I'll help her! Can I, Mom?
That'll help Tía earn enough to buy Christmas gifts!

You're so wonderful, my mom says.

Naaah, piece o' cake. I smile.
And I mean it.

After all, how hard
can babysitting a five-year-old be?

JADE

Jade is five and acts like my shadow.
She wants to read everything I write
and copy everything I do
and hear everything I say
(especially when I'm on the phone with Liz or Cata).
It's kind of flattering that she loves me so much,
but sometimes she sponges up all my attention
until I think I'm being sucked into
a big black hole in space!
She asks me at least fifty questions
about kittens and kangaroos and turtles
till my head's spinning.
Then she gives me a big hug and says,
You look like Wonder Woman! Here's a cape!
and I laugh. I love her so much and try to be patient
and give her lots of attention.

I think I'll write her a poem,
just so she has something else to read
OTHER than these scribbles
in my purple notebook
that USED to be private.

THE MAMA WHO DOESN'T LIKE PETS
(to Jade)

I wanted a turtle.
My mama said no.
I begged for a gerbil.
She just shook her head.
I asked for a parrot.
Her voice just growled low.
I pled for a lizard.
Her face turned beet red.

I saw a cute Chihuahua
and a fox terrier too!
I swore to pay for food and vet.
(I've got cash saved—I do!)
But Mama just refuses.
(I don't know why.)
I guess she just hates animals.
She doesn't even try!

So I just sit here lonely
with my goldfish and three cats,
my fluffy cocker spaniel
and two kangaroo rats,
my black furry bunny
and my noisy cockatiels
while Mama feeds the monkeys
and picks up banana peels.

Then she walks the alligator
and feeds the kangaroo.
I guess she just hates animals.
I think she does, don't you?

AGAIN, DEAR MR. MASON

Today in the library, I found a special book
and decided to write to Mr. Mason about it.

Dear Mr. Mason—
I just read a book about Emma Tenayuca.
It's a history book about the life of a young girl
like me, who grew up here in this city.
Have you read it? She fought for justice and
made speeches about workers' low wages and long hours
and lack of running water. When the owners didn't listen,
she helped the workers organize a strike.
And she didn't back down when they threw her in jail
or said ugly things about her.
She cared about the people, ALL the people,
especially the ones who had no voice, no money, no power.
Even those who had no papers.
And when they won the strike,
it made headlines all over the world!
And I loved that book. And I loved the heroine.
And she was real.
Like me.
Why doesn't *SHE* show up in our history book?
Why can't we read more stories about people like her?
About brown women activists like my gramma.
Why aren't Gramma's stories about protesting for equal rights
in the Chicano movement included in our textbooks?

But thanks for letting us have free time in the library,
because I love the library
and I'm glad it includes at least SOME of our stories.
And by the way, I decided
I really do want to be a historian
so I can tell more of the stories that need telling.
I just have one question.
How do I start?
From,
Celina Teresa Guerrera Amaya

GOOD WILL TO ALL

This morning, everywhere I turn
there's holiday music playing.
All happy songs of Peace and Love
and Good Will to All
and Joy to the World.
Really? To the WHOLE world?
You mean it?
Because if you really believe in Good Will to All,
you're gonna have to change the way
you treat people who are different from you.
And if not, then say what you mean:
good will to
some.

OTHER CALENDARS, OTHER CELEBRATIONS

I learned from my gramma to love celebrations,
to respect holiday traditions wherever I go.
Diwali, Eid, Ramadan, Rosh Hashanah, Hannukah,
Kwaanza, Christmas, Solstice, Día de los Reyes—
all like different jewels in a treasure chest.

I thought I knew all the holidays of the year,
but I find there are other calendars, not just ours.
The Egyptians had a calendar, and the Chinese,
the Mayans and the Persians and the Aztecs too.

And if *they* all had a calendar, *I* can have
a calendar too—with all the days important to *me*.
If *their* heroes' birthdays are holidays,
then I can add holidays for *my* heroes too—
and let people know all about them.

So this year, on December 21,
I'm celebrating the birthday of
Emma Tenayuca because I think it's right
to celebrate those
who fight for justice
and who are brave and kind,
who fight to defend the people who have money
and those who don't.
Those who speak English
and those who don't.

Those who have papers
and those who don't.
I think *she* would have fought to help my dad too,
and even to help *me* have *my* history
included in school.

TO EMMA TENAYUCA, ON HER BIRTHDAY

Dear Emma—
How come I never knew who you were until now?
How come they didn't put you in my history book?
You stood on the steps of City Hall
and raised your brave voice and your clenched fist
and told the whole world that NO workers
should have to work sixty hours a week and
still not make enough to feed their families,
like the thousands of pecan-shellers in San Antonio.
You fought for everyone—the poor, the young,
the people with no papers.
And you left us words about why and how we fight.
Words like, *If you fight with hatred,*
your fight for justice cannot survive.
You have to have love
for a cause.

So I'll have a piece of cake to celebrate your life.
I'll crack a pecan and shell it too,
to remember you and the tired, hungry workers
who fought, with love, beside you.
And since your spirit is still with us,
I'll invite EVERYONE to join in this, YOUR celebration,
and share their piece of cake, their gifts, their life,
their love with everyone.

TAMALADAS AND THE LAST 8,000 YEARS!

I thought we'd done everything we needed for Christmas.
Hung lights, prepared gifts, wrapped presents.
Went to a Posadas celebration,
where a big group of friends
walked to nine different houses,
singing at each to please let us in,
like Mary and Joseph, looking for the inn,
until the ninth house finally sang back to come on in.
We'd even baked buñuelos and put up a tree!

But then Gramma says, ¡¡¡Tamalada!!!
and prepares to turn our house into
an assembly line.
I whine, *Again? Like last year?*
Tamaladas mean so much WORRRRK!
Gramma just smiles. *You like fast food?*
Tamales were the first fast food on this continent.
And they come in a disposable, recyclable wrapper!
They are like centuries of wisdom.
They sneak their way into your soul.
They help create your community, your team,
bring people together to talk and laugh, share sorrows,
solve problems, lighten each other's loads.
The people of these Américas have been making (and eating)
tamales for eight thousand years!
I'm still pouting.

And then she says,
It doesn't need to be just MY comadres.
You can invite YOUR friends too!
And THAT
changes everything!

TAMALES ARE FOREVER!

On Saturday, the tamalada happens!
I invite Liz, Cata, Chato—and Heather too!
Each of us are assigned stations.
Some lay out the hojas, and others work the masa.
Some spread the masa on the shucks,
and others fill them with meat or beans
(or with our histories or with our dreams!).
Gramma lays the tamales in the pot
like a tall pyramid standing up just right.
Twenty dozen!
And we laugh when the one she puts on top
has a little bow tie made of strips of corn shucks.

While the pots begin to clank and bubble,
while the steam drifts up like the spirits of the grammas
who made them just like this millennia ago,
and the aroma fills the kitchen like love,
we all sing and talk, clean and wait,
till they're finally ready, and we all feast at last.

Then everyone, with hearts and tummies full,
sighs and gives abrazos before heading back home.
Each carrying their small bundle of homemade tamales
and 8,000 years of history
to share with THEIR families too.

Gramma was right.
Magic tamales, gift-wrapped with a bow,
steamed their aromas
right into my soul.

THE POWER TO CONNECT US

Chato was so excited on Monday morning,
he could hardly wait to tell me how his little brothers
gobbled the tamales up.
And Heather's story was just the same!
(Except it was her parents and teenage sister who
did the gobbling.)
And everybody was so proud that they
had helped make the tamales themselves—
and they asked if they could help every year!
Umm, YES!

*I felt like we were so connected, like we were all part
of the same family. Who knew making tamales
could be so much fun?* Liz giggles.

Well, I knew eating them would be! shouts Cata.

I LET MS. YÁÑEZ SEE MY EMMA TENAYUCA POEM

When I show Ms. Yáñez my Emma Tenayuca poem,
her eyes get big.
This woman is an icon, Ms. Yáñez says,
and you painted her portrait beautifully with your poem
to her—more people should see this.

Yeah, I say. *Everyone should know about Emma.*

But I didn't know Ms. Yáñez would show my poem
to Ms. Bermea, my cool Spanish teacher,
who loved it and asked me if she could share it
with her eighth graders when they discuss
Mexican American history in San Antonio.
And then Ms. Bermea suggested to Mr. Mason that he
could use it in his unit on civil rights leaders in February.
(And he showed it to Mr. Vega, who only teaches science,
so at least I know we won't hear anything about it there.
Whew!)

But on the last day of school before the holidays,
Mr. Vega beams his big funny smile and says,
I want to wish everybody a very merry . . .
EMMA TENAYUCA'S BIRTHDAY tomorrow!
And if you don't know who she is,
you're missing out on a great SHE-ro!
So go check the poem posted on the hallway bulletin board,
and tomorrow, enjoy a piece of cake for me!

Better yet, stick it in the freezer and bring ME
that piece of cake in January!
¡Adió-ó-ó-ó-ós!

Wow! It's amazing how many people you can reach with a poem!

DECEMBER CAN BE HARD

While it's great to be off for the holidays
and stay up late watching movies
and see relatives I don't always get to see,
I miss seeing my classmates—I even miss going to class!
And I remember that our school counselor
said holidays *can be stressful to those who've*
experienced a loss.
And I know that means me, because
missing your dad so much that
your stomach feels like a beat-up lemon
that's squished and splattered in a molcajete
sure feels like a loss.
And Liz is in church services tonight
and Cata isn't answering the phone
and Chato went to Mexico
to see his grandfather.
And it's hard to figure things out sometimes
when you don't have your friends
to talk to.

A PLAN OF ACTION

Tía and Jade come over for Christmas Day,
and it feels so good to have them here.
Jade carries her new purple guitar with her everywhere,
and now she's giving Mom and Gramma a concert in the den.

Tía is sitting with me in the kitchen, and I think about how
I never see her down.
She always says, *Why worry?*
Worry never makes a solution.
What we need here is a plan of action.
I used to laugh at this every time she said it,
but now I find myself wondering what
plan of action might get rid of MY worry.

I ask Tía if she thinks Jade misses her dad
the way I miss mine,
and Tía says it's different for Jade—
She was never used to seeing him that much,
whereas you remember having a dad almost
every day of your life, and a really great dad.
Actually, Jade loves and misses her tío, your dad.
The way he picked her up and carried her on his shoulders
and swung her around the way daddies do.

My face must tell Tía how sad and worried I am,
because all of a sudden she blurts out,

You wanna go for a ride to see the Christmas lights
in the other neighborhoods?
And we do.

I like having an aunt with a plan of action!

SENDING DAD A MESSAGE ON THE WINGS OF HOPE

Right before we left for the holidays,
Ms. Yáñez gave me a book of poems
she said I might enjoy.
The poems are by Emily Dickinson.
One is called "'Hope' is the thing with feathers."
It sounds weird, but it makes sense
in that way that poems do.
When we have hope, it carries us up
as if we can fly above the problems.
Dad, I agree with Ms. Dickinson.
Hope is the thing with feathers.
And
my feathers

all fly

to you.

BEAUTIFUL DARK BROWN

It's Mom's day off from work,
and we're celebrating with a treat!
Mom is taking me and Jade to Natural Foods,
where they have everything imaginable to eat,
even an ice cream deli.
Jade and I choose pizza to start, and when
Mom lays the slices down on the table in our booth,
Jade finally puts her guitar down to eat.
Then Mom remembers she needs to make a call.
I'll be right back. Don't move! she says, and I nod.

Jade sees a little blond girl alone at a nearby table
and jumps up. *I'm gonna give her a concert!*
Before I can even stop her, she's playing her guitar,
and the little girl smiles. *Mama, look!*
A lady runs over and grabs the guitar out of Jade's hands.
How DARE you take my baby's guitar! You people!
Then she looks at me and says, *Stealing is wrong.*
Didn't your mother teach you kids that?

Before I can open my mouth, the little girl says,
Mommy! Mine is in the cart. The woman looks, turns bright red.
And without a moment's hesitation, I say,
Judging people by their color is wrong!
Didn't YOUR mother ever teach you that?

Her mouth drops as she hands the guitar back to Jade.
Oh, I'm so sorry. Please forgive me.
The lady grabs her daughter's hand
and runs off as fast as she can.

Jade and I sit back down, kind of in shock.
But when I think about how I took action, it makes me smile.
Some people sure are clueless, I tell Jade. And then I add,
Did anyone ever tell you that you have
the most beautiful dark brown skin?
And she gives me the most sparkling happy smile right back.

A WHOLE NEW YEAR!

It's January, the big Number One month!
Each year, a brand-new start
filled with dreams
where anything can happen,
where luck can land, and I hope it does.
My mom says, *For good luck in the new year,*
eat twelve grapes at midnight on New Year's Eve,
one grape for each month of the year!
My tía says, *Wear new chones under your clothes!*
Even though no one else can see them,
YOU'LL know you're starting the new year fresh,
inside and out.
My gramma says, *The black-eyed peas simmering*
on the stove will bring us all good luck!

So I sit here eating grapes and black-eyed peas
and hoping that we'll have good luck and
all our dreams come true.

After all, in a few weeks it'll be MLK Day,
when my whole city joins in a giant march.
For us, that also starts Dream Week,
when we celebrate Dr. King's vision
and try to keep his dreams for a better future
alive.

I believe when people dream, it's like a holy state.

And we should respect that sacred space
inside of everyone
where dreams
can bloom.

THE MAGIC WORD

I'm glad to be back in school with all my friends.
The hallways are filled with a buzz of excitement
as the day gets colder and cloudier outside
and someone whispers, like a prayer, the magic word:
SNOW! And our hearts race at even the thought.
Yes, I said *snow*. That cold white powdery stuff
that falls from the sky and makes the world magical.
That seems to fall almost EVERYwhere.
Except here.
Here it gets cold. Or it gets hot. It floods. Or it hails.
Or it's windy. Or perfectly sunny.
But once every handful of years it really DOES snow here!
Just enough to keep the dream alive.
And that dream picks me up a little when I'm down,
and makes me remember a winter years ago when my family
was all together, happy, playing, in our little tiny pile of
snow.

FREEDOM

I wish I was free to fly all over the world
and find my dad and bring him home.
I wish he was free
to live in any country he wanted to,
whether or not he had the money
to pay lawyers to get
the papers people judge you by.

Dr. King said it's your character that counts.
Not where you were born,
or your accent, your faith, your color.
Character.
He said it brave, he said it true.
Kept saying it no matter what they'd do to him.
Laid his whole life down to build it,
pay it, keep it
precious
for us.

Freedom—
it's either there for everyone
or it isn't there
at all.

SOCIAL JUSTICE

Ms. Yáñez is talking about social justice
and about the speeches of MLK.
How he argued for justice.
How he fought for fair chances.

Can you think of other civil rights leaders
who've used speeches and writing to demand justice?
César Chávez, says Liz.
Dolores Huerta, says Cata. *She organized farmworkers too!*
Emma Tenayuca! I shout.

And as I say it, something bright blares loud inside me.
Emma Tenayuca, Dolores Huerta, and MLK were warriors.
And I was named Guerrera, warrior, for a reason.
Because I was MEANT to be a warrior too,
a freedom fighter, love-for-a-cause Warrior!
Meant to be! And AM!
Fighting with my weapons—paper and pen.
Using my courage to speak up.
Using celebration spirit to keep me strong
so I never give up.
Because guerreras never stop
fighting for what they believe in.

SOLO LO BARATO

There are Valentine hearts in all the store windows.
And big, beautiful cards.
Red-as-red-can-be,
can't-take-your-eyes-off-me
shiny cards that I wanted so badly when I was little.
Gramma, why wasn't I born rich? I asked her back then.
Solo lo barato se compra con dinero. She'd sigh.
Which means, Only cheap things
can be bought with money.
I wasn't sure what she meant then, but I know now.
The best kind of hearts are the ones that smile, listen,
cheer you up, sit beside you in the cafeteria.

My dad said that in Mexico, Valentine's is also called
Friends Day. And I'm lucky to have THREE great friends!
Liz helps me understand what I feel. Cata makes me laugh.
Chato helps me be strong when things are tough.
So those are the hearts that *this* guerrera
will be celebrating on February 14.
And they are worth way more than any shiny card.

BLACK LIVES MATTER!

Cata is angrier than I've ever heard her.
They SHOT him! she says. Just SHOT him!

Who?

Ahmaud Arbery! I just saw it on the news.
Another Black man. Shot!
They can't keep profiling Blacks this way.
Black Lives Matter! As much as any other person's.
Do you know how many this makes?

The thought of someone being shot for just jogging
makes me shiver.
Cata's furious. She sounds like I did last summer
after the El Paso shooter killed so many people
in a Walmart just because they were Mexican.

When will this stop? How many more will it take?
Remember, Celi, what your MLK poem said: "Freedom—
it's either there for EVERYONE
or it isn't there at all."

She's quoting my "Freedom" poem!
I gave her a copy and she memorized it?
Do words really have that much power?

ERASED AND IGNORED

So there's this teacher who always pronounces
my last name *Grrr-Uh*
even though I tell her it's *Geh-RARE-rah.*
And she never pays attention to Chato
when he raises his hand to ask for help in math.
So today I was standing in front of the lockers
getting my notebook for afternoon classes,
and some loud girl at a nearby locker
was cussing out her "friend" and threatening,
I'll hit you so hard they'll take you to the HOSPITAL
. . . if you're still ALIVE!

Math Teacher hears the commotion and comes
running out—toward ME!
She's shouting, *Young lady, you stop that behavior immediately!*
Before I can say anything, she's on this walkie-talkie
to the principal's office, telling him, *We've got a*
fight in the northwest hallway by room 207.
And when me and Liz and Chato try
to tell her it wasn't me, she ignores us.
Loud Girl keeps laughing and points a finger at me, saying,
Yeah, ma'am, I bet Mexican Girl was gonna pull a knife on me!
And Math Teacher keeps looking at me like I'M the criminal.
But it was HER shouting, I try to explain, and again
this teacher doesn't hear me. Doesn't hear me at all.

CLEAN-CUT

So Math Teacher is still holding on to me
when another teacher starts running
toward us and, all out of breath, gasps,
That girl over there was the one shouting,
not the one you're holding.
And Math Teacher lets go of me, with a blank look on her face,
and just says, *Oh.* And to the walkie-talkie, *Never mind.*
Then she walks up to Loud Girl
and just says quietly, *Don't do that again, okay?*
Now get to class.

A minute later, Loud Girl is hurrying to her class
and Math Teacher is explaining to Out-of-Breath Teacher,
She must have been provoked. I know her. Clean-cut.
Comes from a good family.

Liz and Chato and I just watch in shock.
Then the bell rings,
we run, and I don't see either of them
till after fifth period.
But all through PE, I feel like I'm gonna cry.
By the time we're together again,
in sixth-period math,
I'm breathing slow and deep like an angry bull.
Liz fumes, *I can't believe she would just automatically*
assume WE were the troublemakers!
Chato looks down and mumbles, *I can.*

And Ms. Math Teacher?
She just conducts class like normal
and doesn't meet my eyes, not even once.
It's like I'm invisible. Or even worse.
When it comes to anything except trouble,
I don't exist at all.

DON'T LET IT IN

What did Ms. Jackson mean by
clean-cut? I ask.
White, Chato states flatly.

Well, maybe she was just confused, says Heather,
who's joined us at our lockers at the end of the day.
She's always been nice to me.

Nice to YOU, says Chato.
Have you ever wondered why she calls on you
every time you raise your hand?

You mean she doesn't call on you? Heather asks.
Not once this whole year. Chato seethes.
I can wave my hand for thirty minutes
and she won't even look my way.

And she certainly wasn't nice to Celi today, snaps Liz.
She was WRONG
and she should've apologized!

Heather looks thoughtful. *Maybe it's 'cause those girls*
go to her same church and she knows them?
I see them there together all the time.

Nah, Chato says. *I think it's about color.*

Some colors she trusts, and others
she doesn't.

Heather's mouth is open.
But that's just like those men who thought the jogger-guy,
Arbery, was a criminal, just because of his color!
And Liz and Chato and I just look at her and nod.

I'm still shaking when I get home.
I think about Gramma's shield.
To stay strong, remember who you are.
What they say can't hurt you if you don't let it in.

But every now and then,
I guess even the best shield
gets a little crack in it.

I'VE GOT HOMEWORK TONIGHT

I've got lots of homework tonight,
but I don't feel like doing it.
I should start on my big report,
but I don't feel like writing it.

Mama's got the night off, asks,
Wanna watch our favorite show?
I just shrug and stay slumped
on the porch, staring out.

Sometimes we're not at our best
and some little voice grumbles so low
we can't even hear it grumbling,

but still, it messes with
the song we'd like to be singing,
the life we'd like to be living.

I wish I knew
what that grumbly little voice
was saying.

Maybe then
I could answer
it back.

CINNAMON DOESN'T LOOK THE SAME

Daddy always called me his cinnamon girl,
and I always loved it.
But I guess not everyone likes cinnamon.
Color of skin seems such a silly reason to judge someone,
or for laws to be made that are stricter for brown people
immigrating from Mexico than for white people
immigrating from Canada or Europe.

I'm not even as dark as lots of my friends.
Do they get suspected, blamed, and called names more?

And what about little Jade?
I've always loved her beautiful dark brown skin,
but that lady at Natural Foods didn't!
What'll happen to her when SHE goes to school?

I'd better watch over Jade like a hawk.
Like a guerrera hawk!
But I'm scared. How in the world
can I protect her from
everything?

LOOKING FORWARD

Lots of days we meet with Ms. Yáñez before school,
to go over plans for our
Making Our World More Fair.

*There's so much to do to make
real change happen around this place.* I sigh.
Liz lays an understanding hand
on my shoulder,
and Ms. Yáñez nods her head.
Their support makes me feel stronger,
allows me to breathe deeper.

I sent invitations to all the city council, Cata chirps.
*And the PTA has put us on their calendar, so
all the parents should know.*

I'm working on my welcome speech, reports Liz.
*And we have three more students who've agreed
to read a poem or story. Plus, I heard Ms. Bermea is
giving her class extra points if they attend.*

Chato proudly announces, *The posters are almost ready.*
I join in, *Chato and Liz have created
beautiful displays
for the people to view when they arrive,
while the seventh-grade mariachi band is playing.*

We're all beaming with hope.
Emma Tenayuca said that even little changes
make a difference, and it's true.
We're feeling it. It's happening.
We are going to make this place better!
And something inside me breathes freer.

TEAM SPIRIT

I scoot to class as fast as I can, and Heather
comes running to catch up with me, jumping for joy.
This Friday is St. Patrick's Day!!!

No, it's not. St. Patrick's Day is the seventeenth.

*Yes, but that's during Spring Break, so they're letting us
do it on Friday, right before Spring Break!
You HAVE to wear green Friday! Don't forget, okay?*

But I'm not Irish, Heather.

That doesn't matter, she says.
*We're all a little Irish on St. Patrick's Day!
Just to be part of team spirit!*

Hmmm. *YOUR team,* I'm thinking,
and I begin to feel irritated. She's so sure *her*
history is important for *everyone* to celebrate,
but *my* history still keeps getting erased.

Then I think of what Gramma says about teaching others,
and of how Emma Tenayuca was patient enough
to negotiate answers.
If we want our world to be more fair,
we have to be ready to explain and discuss.

OKAY, I'll wear green Friday IF
you promise to wear red, white, and green
on Cinco de Mayo.

What's Cinco de Mayo?
I explain that it's May 5, when Mexican troops
overthrew the French occupation of their land
over a hundred and fifty years ago,
but now it's mostly to celebrate Mexican spirit and culture.

Sure, she says. *That sounds fun.*
And somehow, the world around me
feels just a little bit
more fair.

NOT TO WORRY

Dad *still* isn't back
and it's been almost seven months now.
Mom said not to worry
(but she looks worried).
Please let him be safe in Mexico.
I keep reading about all these people
who asked for asylum
but are locked in crowded cages at the border
and not given court dates for months and months
or maybe not at all.
And our hearts are starting to sink with worry,
wondering if Dad's okay.

But now we've got something else
to worry about

as if we didn't
have enough
already.

WHAT'S A PANDEMIC?

I used to get allergies a lot,
and I sometimes suffer with sniffles.
Now there's something way worse than allergies,
something worse than sniffles,
something so tiny you don't see it coming.
But so big it can knock you down
and make it a struggle just to walk
or stand
or breathe.

A tiny spiky little virus
is killing people across the whole planet.
In our country, almost a thousand people
DIED of it in just one day!

And while at first I thought it was fun when school closed,
now we don't go anywhere or do anything.
I never thought I'd get bored from NOT having school.
I never thought I'd even miss PE and hearing Coach Windrider say,
Let's do another set of hamstring stretches!
I never thought I'd miss the sound of traffic and honking horns.
But I do. Everything is so quiet.
Way, way too quiet.

WHEN THINGS ARE TOUGH

Gramma always says, *When things are tough,*
count your blessings.

So, ONE: I'm thankful I have my gramma
alive and well.
Able to stay home
to not get infected.

TWO: I have a mom who's out there helping.
She's staying careful even though she has to
work nights at the clinic and has to throw all her clothes
in the washing machine and take a shower
the minute she gets home,
before she can hug me.

THREE: I still *have* a school,
even though it's going to be online for a while.
And I'll have lots of good books to read
that the teacher will put online.

FOUR: I'm thankful we have a phone
and my friends can call me
and I can still hear their voices
after school hours.

And FIVE: that I don't have a cough.
And I do have soap and water.

And we have a thermometer.
And no one has a fever here.

And hopefully a SIX: that Dad is fine.
And safe? That wherever he is,
he has soap and water
and hopefully
a mask.

FLASHLIGHT

Liz calls me while her little brothers
are taking a nap. And even SHE sounds down.

What's the matter? I ask.

The beach, she sighs. *Remember the beach?*

The trip to the beach! Your family vacation? Oh no.
You can't go, right?

Right. The beaches are closed. The parks are closed.
It feels like the whole world is closed!
And they say it could be a year or TWO before there's
a vaccine to protect us from COVID.
A year or two without the beach!

I'm sorry, Liz, I say, and I try to think of something to help.
Maybe . . . you could hook up that water slide game?
And splash in your brothers' kiddie pool?
And close your eyes to some online recording
of "Sounds of Ocean Waves"?

Done that.

Really? I laugh. *I sure wish I'd seen that!*
Hey, how about you find an online book or a movie about
some ocean adventure or something on a tropical island?

Done that too.

Wow! I'm impressed, Liz!

Can I tell you a secret, Celi? It wasn't just me seeing the beach.
My family had promised that we could invite you!
So I'd dreamed of three days at the beach where you and I
laughed and swam and built castles with moats
and stayed up late with our flashlights, telling scary stories,
and we'd come back and have a trip we would
laugh about and remember forever.

I try to comfort Liz, but I feel awful for all she's missing—
all I'm missing now too.
Liz, I tell her. *Let's still do PART of that.*
Over the phone or on FaceTime.
We can tell scary stories. And dream wild dreams.
And tell each other everything.
Nothing can stop us from being there
for each other.

Celi, thanks for being you.
You're like my own flashlight:
full of light and bright ideas!

And the next morning I see our mailbox has a big package
stuffed inside it—and when I open it I see
a book of scary stories, signed *TO CELI,*
for FRIDAY NIGHT! along with a flashlight
and a pair of beach sandals
that are just my size!

IN CASE OF EMERGENCY

Gramma has always kept extra cans of food
and a tiny box of cash stashed away.
In case of emergency,
she said.

I thought she was silly to save stuff
we could be using now, but she'd said,
We have plenty to meet our needs.
It's good to think ahead
to when there might not be so much
so readily available, so easy to get.

So she would save old blankets to be sewn into quilts.
And old boxes to store things we might need someday,
like old jeans and shoelaces, elastic, old sheets.

Now Gramma is cutting up old sheets and shoelaces
to sew masks for us to wear.
And Mama is making tortillas from masa harina,
not from the store ready-bought,
'cause we try not to go inside stores very often.
And now I think I understand how smart Gramma really is.
Because now—is a REAL
"case of emergency."

TOILET PAPER

Cata calls to say, *Want to hear a bummer?*
Stores are running out of toilet paper!

Whaaaat??? Are you kidding me, Cata?
Even toilet paper is hard to get?

So much has changed.
It was already weird when we had to wash our hands
every time we touched ANYthing. And now?
We won't WANT to touch anything!!!

Then Mama comes home and says she had to check five stores
before she could find one that had a four-pack of toilet paper.
And the next time I go to the store with her,
it looks like a ghost town on lots of the shelves.
One aisle had just two cans of spinach
sitting alone there like outcasts
shipwrecked on a desert island.

On the news they're saying that the virus is really tough
on people over sixty-five.
And Gramma is sixty-eight.
But Gramma's SUPER strong!
No little old virus can mess with her!
(Can it?)

It was better
when all I had to worry about
was running out
of toilet paper.

WHAT IF?

The restaurants and taco trucks have posted CLOSED signs,
and the stores lock their doors early at night.
We're told to stay home another week after Spring Break.
Then we're told don't come back to school for two more weeks.
And then we're told we'll do classes online till the end of the year!

The days seem awfully long
since we have to "stay home and stay safe."
I miss Liz's slow smile and quiet voice.
I miss Cata's loud, happy laugh.
I miss Chato's jokes and his kind ways.
I miss seeing Tía and little Jade.

Now everyone is worried.
What if someone has to go to the hospital
and they run out of hospital beds,
like some experts are predicting might happen?
What if the people who pick our food get sick
and there are no avocados or tomatoes?
That means there's no more guacamole.
And no one to make the chips?
Or even the bread? Or peanut butter?
Or to deliver the flour to the store to make flour tortillas?
What if all the farmers get sick and close the farms?

My head is exploding with so many questions.
And my stomach's scrunching up.

So I decide I can't worry about everything.
But I CAN wash my hands
and wear my mask
and stand six feet away from others if I have to go out.

Sometimes you just do
what you can.

CHANGES

A lotta lotta changes have happened
that are hard to adjust to.
Like not seeing friends or even family.
When I see little Jade, it's from a distance.
Just a tiny hand waving from the back seat of Tía's car.

But the biggest change now
is that every country on the planet
is fighting the same war.
All of us on the same side.
All of us with the same enemy.
All of us wondering how an enemy so tiny
can make us all stay inside and hide.

WHAT WE DON'T ALWAYS KNOW ABOUT OUR FRIENDS

I was so bored about not going anywhere
that I jumped on my bike and rode around the neighborhood.
Not very exciting. But suddenly, I saw Chato
on his bike and I waved and stopped six feet away from him
(social distancing)
to ask how he was doing.
He said he was helping his mom by
selling her pan dulce to gas station convenience stores
so they could make a little money to buy food.
He looked worried. And maybe hungry.
There were four empanadas
in a package in his bike basket
that hadn't been sold.
I told him, *My gramma loves empanadas!*
Can we buy what you have left?
So he followed me home and waited while
I brought the money out to the porch,
along with a big food container from my gramma.

What's this? he asked.
Fideo con pollo, I answered.
My gramma made a huge pot of it
and wanted to share.

And suddenly, a big sunshiny smile
broke out on his face
as if I'd handed him a treasure box.

My four little brothers are gonna LOVE this!

I didn't know he had *four* brothers.
I didn't know he was still out working
despite the quarantine.
I didn't know his family was worried about
not having enough food.
But what I do know now
is that Chato is very caring and responsible
and has a VERY
nice smile.

POEM TO CÉSAR CHÁVEZ, ON HIS BIRTHDAY, MARCH 31

Today we celebrate your birthday, César Chávez.
When you were a boy, you and your family worked hard
in the fields from sunup to sundown.
But no matter how hard your parents worked,
they never earned enough for the family's needs.
Food. Medicine. Blankets. Shoes.
You saw the injustice, and as you grew,
you worked to change things so that farmworkers
would have a union and a voice.
You fought with courage and kindness.
You touched the earth and cultivated its best—
like the sun, which shines equally on everyone.

We can't have the César Chávez march this year,
but I can read about your life and your struggles.
And remember the farmworkers who, even today,
while we stay home, are still working, still sweating,
still harvesting our food.
They call them "frontline workers."
They're keeping us
alive.

NATIONAL POETRY MONTH

Ms. Yáñez told us
that April is National Poetry Month
and that we'll read a poem every day
this month by a different poet.

She started with a poem by a Chicana writer
who grew up on the same street I live on!
And even just the first verse felt like a gift.

Never write with pencil,
m'ija.
It is for those
who would
erase.
Make your mark proud
and open,
Brave,
beauty folded into
its imperfection,
Like a piece of turquoise
marked.

I remember seeing this poem on a poster on the bus,
and liking that it uses the word *m'ija*,
'cause it feels like she's talking straight to me.
The poem told me I'm free to be me.
And proud of it.

Without apologizing
or trying to erase myself
or to undo my name
or my language
or my feelings.
That's what this poem
means to me.

LAUGHTER IS A WEAPON TOO

The teachers are struggling to make our virtual lessons
more interesting and keep us engaged.
But some kids aren't tuning in, and others are half asleep.
Those teachers should talk to our science teacher, Mr. Vega.
He used to be funny. But now? He's a blast!
Some days he gets dressed up
and acts the experiments out.
Yesterday, he acted like he was Isaac Newton
and an apple fell on his head!
And at the end of each lesson, he does "True Confessions:
Little Secrets You Need to Know about Science."
Today he said, *I know you'd think, from our textbooks,*
that scientists are all white men.
True Confessions: They're not. Our books don't tell you
about all the women scientists,
or the scientists who were people of color.
Hopefully new books will be written
before I turn into an old man
that tell their stories too.
Books that tell the truth.
And THE TRUTH SHALL SET YOU FREEEEE! he bellowed.

We all laughed at that. But we remembered what he said.
Looks like someone needs to start adding stuff to our science books.
(Hopefully not me. The science might turn out upside down.
Maybe Liz? Yeah, Liz could write a GOOD science book!)

I WON'T GET TO FLY A KITE THIS YEAR

This year I won't get to fly a kite or hunt for Easter eggs
or crack cascarones at the park
where we usually have an Easter picnic with
Gramma and lots of aunts and uncles and cousins,
and Dad.

This year the parks are closed
and we're still under *stay home and stay safe* rules.

Easter will just be Mom and Gramma and me
in the backyard with some tacos and watermelon.
And now I'll miss more people than just Dad.
But I can still dream
right here in my quarantine chrysalis.
And when I get so bored because we can't do anything,
I can write about celebrations the way they USED to be.

So I'll write a poem about kites
to make Jade laugh.
Just to make it feel more like
we're all still
together.

FIESTA'S REAL ROYALTY

Fiesta is my favorite holiday
in San Antonio
because the whole city joins in
to celebrate.
There's a parade floating down our river,
and even a King Fido parade for dogs.
(Can you imagine a King Papita Frita?)
There's a nighttime Fiesta Flambeau
and a Night in Old San Antonio.
But the best part of all is that
EVERYONE is royalty in this great city.
Everyone wears crowns of flowers.
And wears sashes with shiny medallions
that proclaim:
Her Royal Highness, Mary Esther,
Queen of the Air Conditioner!
or brag **The Baron of Burritos!**
or **The Royal Order of the Janitors!**
The Marquesa of Mayonesa!
and **The Duchess of the Glitter Glue Gun.**
Everybody gets into the Fiesta Fun,
cracking cascarones and trading medals.
And everybody feels Super Important
and Super Valuable because
in this city where people value each other,
Fiesta's REAL Royalty is us.

So even though there'll be
no parades this year,
we'll all stay home and do it gladly.
Because ROYALTY shouldn't get others sick.
And REAL ROYALTY cares about EVERYONE.

THE ONLY THING TO MAKE US FEEL BETTER

Liz sets up a virtual meeting for us on the day
that would have been our Making Our World More Fair.
We're all so disappointed and the only thing to make us
feel better is seeing each other, even virtually.
Cata pops up on our screens wearing SIX Fiesta medallions.
They're from last year. She shrugs.
But hey, you gotta do what you can do.

I hope you're writing a lot, Celi, says Cata. *'Cause, híjole,*
we sure need your good words.
This is the QUIETEST Fiesta I can remember,
and, unfortunately, I got a good memory.

It's sooo hard not getting together, I say,
but I do keep writing about things to celebrate and
things to fight for . . . if they ever get a chance to be heard.

They will someday! says Liz. *But for now—what can we celebrate?*

Earth Day's coming right up, and it's important!
'Cause we're trashing up the planet! Cata shakes her head.
My tía's really angry at the corporations adding to global warming.
She says the LAST thing we need is for summer to get any HOTTER!
Or we'll literally fry.

Really, every day should be Earth Day, Liz says.
My brother Roberto gets asthma real bad when the pollution's high.

Maybe we could help the people registering voters
so the laws can change to protect Earth better.
And maybe someone needs to write something inspiring
so we can spread the word around.
Celi?

EARTH DAY
A *POEM SUBMITTED TO THE* SAN ANTONIO EXPRESS-NEWS *POETRY COLUMN*
By Celina Teresa Guerrera Amaya, age 12

Dear Earth,
Have you always been this beautiful?
I'm lying on the grass in my backyard,
and the sky's so blue, the air's so clear.
The birds are delighted, singing, and
one comes and lands near me.
He's dressed in red and sings with all his heart,
like an opera singer in a concert hall.
His audience is me and one other guest
draped in black-and-orange velvet.
A true and graceful monarch, a butterfly.

It's peaceful without the sound of traffic,
like every creature on the planet can breathe more deeply
now that we humans aren't driving and polluting.
Maybe this bird's trying to tell us something,
to ask us who will work to fix the mess we've made.
To save the bees, the whales, the trees,
the sky, the air, the ocean.

Earth, I promise you I'll do my part and
work to get my fellow humans to do theirs too.
My gramma says, *To every creature, every thing,*
we need to give respeto.

And Earth, I want us ALL to give you
loving care and gratitude,
but most of all to give you
the respect
you are due.

LOSING HOPE

It's hard to stay hopeful
when there's so much going wrong in the world.
I'm so tired of hearing people say
they need to build a wall to keep Mexicans away.
And now they're blaming other countries for the *virus*.
And some people are beating up Asians, blaming *them*!
Why does everything have to be the fault of immigrants?
How many times do we have to repeat that most people here
were once immigrants too?

Don't they know that when they say to us,
Go back to where you came from,
it means we might have to move across town
or a few hours down a river
or over a mountain range
or across the continent
but *they'd* have to cross
a whole ocean?
And don't they know—
this planet belongs to us all?

Am I silly to think I can change things
when I'm just a kid?
I'm not in charge of anything but ME,
and ME is struggling hard just to not lose hope.

I remember telling Liz I don't get mad
because I don't like angry.
Because angry people often blow up.
But maybe sometimes we need to blow up
and shake things up to start to change
our world.

YOUNG BROWN GIRL WITH HER FIST IN THE AIR

I'm looking through old photo albums,
at happy pictures of how everything used to be.
Daddy swinging me at a park; Mama as a bride.
Mama graduating high school;
my grandparents with Mom and Tía as teens,
then as babies. And then,
a picture I don't recognize.
A young woman with her fist in the air,
headband on her forehead, and long straight hair.
Her other hand holds a sign that says BROWN POWER,
and there's something in her eyes
that I've seen somewhere before.
Gramma, who's this?
And Gramma just smiles.
Someone who thought she couldn't make a difference.
Before the rules at school were changed.

I stare at that picture for the longest while
and marvel over my gramma's strength and her kindness too.
If she could change the world she lived in,
then I can change this world too!

AN ENVELOPE IN THE MAIL

The mail came in with an envelope addressed to me.
It was from Ms. Yáñez, and I couldn't wait to see
what she'd sent. Maybe it was some poems?
Or some ideas on ways to change the world.

The Post-it Note was purple,
and she wrote on it in turquoise,
Congratulations, Celi! You DID it!
Thanks for making a difference in our world.
I knew you said you didn't have
a subscription to the paper,
so I decided to send you your own copy
before I announced this at school.

I opened the newspaper that was folded inside,
and it had the poetry column at the top of the page.
The poem was called "Earth Day."
And the author of the poem
was me!

DÍA DEL MAESTRO

Gramma says today is Día del Maestro,
Day of the Teacher, in Mexico.
And I'm so grateful for my good ones this year
(and won't mention my not-so-good one).

Mr. Vega, remember that time at the end of science class
you had us talking about our favorite tacos
and you said, *Well, let's taco 'bout it!*
We cracked up laughing, but you were on a roll, lol,
and before you were done, we were rolling on the floor.
Ya párale, or you'll be the taco the town! You taco lot!
Your taco nenzymes is due tomorrow!
I don't know how you do it, but you always make us feel good.
And learn at the same time!
And lots of the students,
especially that kid with the standing-up hair
who wants to be a comedian someday,
are determined to be just like you, and to find humor in every day!
Or YOU, Ms. Bermea, you make us feel brilliant and biliterate!
You're five feet two, but walk like you're ten feet tall
and have Aztec jade all over your crown.
Mr. Mason, you always listen to what we say
and care about what we think,
as if you think we have something special to teach the world.
(And we do!)
You even sent me notes on how to be a good historian.

And Ms. Windrider, you make us feel we could go
to the Olympics! And maybe even ride the wind!
But when I think about Day of the Teacher,
I think most about YOU, Ms. Yáñez,
because so often
when the world feels dark and hopeless,
you say something that makes us feel
like a bright beam of light just lit up a golden path
and that there's magic glowing inside us.

Mexico's right when they say Day of the Teacher
is as important as Mother's Day. Because y'all nurture
us with learning and feed us with ideas that grow so tall
we don't even know
where they'll end up!

CAN. NOT. BELIEVE.

We haven't even seen justice for Ahmaud Arbery yet
and now ANOTHER Black man was killed!
His name is George Floyd.
Over and over again, we see him beg for his life.
He pleads while some guy in uniform doesn't listen,
just looks away as he kneels on George Floyd's neck,
choking out his breath.
George Floyd calls for his mother in heaven to help him.
The people standing by beg the officer to stop, but he
ignores them.

George Floyd didn't have a gun.
George Floyd wasn't threatening anyone.
George Floyd was suspected
of using a fake $20 bill.
And now he is dead.

His voice ignored. His life snuffed out.
Suffocated to death by the knee
of an officer OF. THE. LAW.
Because of his color.

A teenager took the video
and now it's all over the news,
and people are in the streets, MAD.
I ask, but Mama's scared to let me go join the protest.
Are you scared I'll get COVID even though I'll wear a mask?

Or . . . are you scared they'll hurt me because of MY color?
Mom and Gramma look at each other.
Then Gramma says, *I'll go with her.*
And she does!

I'm sorry, Mr. George Floyd, for
what our world did to you.
When we all marched together, we all shouted,
I can't BREATHE!
And when I think back on all the
erased histories, erased names, and erased lives,
no, I *really* can't breathe either.

MS. YÁÑEZ SAYS WE MIGHT EXPERIENCE STRESS

The school year ended today.
But we weren't able to celebrate that together
since we're all still doing school from home.
Can't see or be with
Liz or Cata,
Chato or Ms. Yáñez.
Or even that kid with the standing-up hair
who always makes bilingual jokes, like
Knock, knock. Who's there? Chata.
Chata who?
Chata Door!
and makes us laugh.

And the news is full of bad things.
COVID deaths, and Black deaths, and shooters
with assault guns,
and still no vaccine or social activities.
And Ms. Yáñez says we might experience stress.
Yeah, Ms. Yáñez?
I *definitely* think we might experience stress!

SUMMERTIME, SORTA

So summer's here, like a quiet lull in a storm
because nothing much is happening
and we still can't go anywhere.
But maybe it's just
the eye of the hurricane.
And I still watch the door.

Still, I get more time with Mom
before she heads to work.
And sometimes we talk,
and sometimes she braids my hair.
And Gramma and I cut roses,
and sometimes at night we catch lightning bugs
and release them
and remember Dad.

And I'm loving having time to pamper my pets,
especially this big fat cat in my lap,
who thinks he's my tiny baby.
And then I have *another* baby to babysit,
well, a little older than a baby, because . . .
Tía's boss tells her she *has to* go back to work.
(*Just wear a mask, it'll all be okay!*) Yikes!
Mama said that since we've all been isolating so long,
we'll be safe for each other in our own little circle.
So now I babysit Jade at my house
three wild, laughing nights a week.

ANOTHER POET IN THE FAMILY

Jade always sees me writing, and now she
wants to be a poet too.
(Glad I inspired SOMEbody!)
So we start writing a few poems together.
Jade insists they have to rhyme even when I
tell her they don't.
But I follow her orders and we mostly
spend a lot of time
laughing at our silly rhymes.

And then Gramma comes over and
puts her round tortilla-warmer basket on Jade's head,
and drapes a big tan towel around her shoulders,
like a cap and gown, and she starts
ta-ta-ta-daaa-ing to "Pomp and Circumstance"
and says we're celebrating Jade's graduation to poethood!

Jade's eyes grow wide,
and I know she's feeling the same way I do
when Gramma makes *me* feel
wonderful.

CAT'S CRADLE SONG

by Jade and Celi

I'm not your mama,
you big, fat cat.
I'm not your mama—
don't you know that?

Your mama has
a lot of fur,
and she can pounce
and she can purr.

Your mama
also thinks it's nice
to spend her free time
hunting mice.
(Yuck!)

I can't meow.
(Can't even sing!)
I'm just a simple
human being!

I don't have a tail
or pointed teeth
or claws that come out,
then hide in their sheath.

I'm not your mama,
you big, fat cat!
I'M NOT YOUR MAMA!!!

...

But YOU don't know that.

I READ THE PAPER

I hardly ever read the newspaper, but today I did.
It wasn't even MY newspaper. It was a few pages
that had been used to wrap some candles we bought.
And when I opened the pages,
I saw a picture
I recognized.

I didn't know.
I'd never thought about why Mr. Mason
wasn't there on Zoom the last week of school.

When I saw it,
my jaw dropped.
Mr. Mason had caught that new virus
on the very last week of school,
and after two weeks in the hospital,
he died.

SOMETHING WRONG

I feel scared.
I feel like I did something wrong.
I don't want to tell Gramma that Mr. Mason died
because I don't want her thinking about how
he was an older person
and so is she . . .
And I don't want to tell Mom either, 'cause she'll worry about
how I feel, and she already has enough to worry about.
I'm even kind of nervous
about telling Liz.
I don't know what to say.
I don't know what I'm supposed to feel.
I don't understand much
about death
or how to deal with loss
or maybe
how to deal with

anything.

TRADITIONS GIVE US TOOLS TO HELP

I think of my gramma.
How she's not afraid of anything.
How she's dealt with so many losses
and still turns it into something as beautiful
as her altar to the dead.
That makes me remember how Día de los Muertos
helps keep the people we love alive in our hearts.

So I find one of my old history papers
that Mr. Mason had graded with a smiley face and an A.
I put it on Gramma's altar de los muertos
and light a candle.
I tell Mr. Mason thanks for being a good listener,
for really caring when I was upset.
For learning—and trying to teach more—about
Indigenous Peoples' Day.
And then I find my shiny metal water bottle and fill it full
of cool water, just like Mr. Mason used to drink between classes,
and I pick an orange flower from the backyard,
and lay them both on the altar.
I think he'd like the way it looks.

SCARY STORIES AT BEDTIME

Jade's into scary stories lately
and asks me to tell her the story
of La Llorona,
who wanders the riverbanks,
crying in a loud wail
and looking for children
she can steal.
I'm not really in the mood, as I'm still
feeling shaky from the news about Mr. Mason.
But Jade insists, so I give in,
and I tell a very gentle version of the story
(so I don't scare her and
so she can still fall asleep).

Then, after she falls asleep,
it's me who gets really scared . . .

REAL SCARY STORY

I'm getting ready for bed when I hear it.
Something way scarier than ghosts or witchy owls,
like La Llorona or La Lechuza. I hear
a dry cough. Then another.
Then another. And my heart sinks.
Is Gramma sick?
Or is it just allergies?
Is Gramma hurting?
Is it The Virus?
Did I give it to her
'cause I ran to get the mail without my mask and grabbed it
right from the mailman's hands?
Did Jade give it to her? Or Tía?
Or that neighbor who came over without a mask?
Will Mama catch it? Will she die?
I sit on my bed, shivering, listening to every nighttime sound.
La Llorona? A cough? A night owl hooting?
Fear in my throat. Icy cold, cold fear.
There's only one fear worse.
Wondering where my dad is
and if he's ever
coming home.

STAY HOME WITH GRAMMA, OKAY?

Gramma's cough is worse.
Mama wants to stay home to take care of her
but is worried about missing work.
We need the money, she says,
sounding like she's apologizing.
No problem, Mom, I'll watch her.

Thanks, Celi—let's hope it's just a cold.
Call me if she gets a fever or if anything changes.
Just tell whoever answers at the clinic to get me.
That it's an emergency.

She'll be okay, I promise,
hoping it's true.

I sit with my notebook and my books
outside Gramma's door
so I can hear right away
if she needs anything
or if she starts feeling worse.
I hope she doesn't.
I hope it's just her allergies.
I hope I don't have to call Mom.

Gramma hasn't coughed for at least ten minutes
so that's a good sign,
right?

WE GOT A MESSAGE

We got a message!
It was from a distant cousin in McAllen,
calling to tell us Dad's okay,
that he'll be coming home as soon as he
can earn bus fare money for the last leg of the trip.

Distant cousin means someone who cares
but someone we don't know very well.
Distant cousin in English they call,
like, *third cousin twice removed*.
But in Mexican families,
we don't remove anyone at all.

Distant cousin, whoever you are, I'm glad you
live on the border, in McAllen, and I'm glad Dad
could get ahold of you, and I know you won't let him
be without a place to stay when he gets there,
even if it's on your living room floor,
BUT WHY COULDN'T YOU FIND OUT MORE?

Why do we still know almost nothing?
Why didn't you give us a number to reach Dad at?
Why can't I have his hugs right now, when
I need them SO VERY MUCH?

I'M THE ONE

So I'm the one who received the message
'cause Mama was at work
and Gramma in bed for the night.

And I'm the one who's supposed to tell Mama
when she gets home from work
tomorrow morning.

And I'm the one
who's supposed to be super
responsible.

But I am also
The One
Who Can't Stand It
Any
More.

I CAN'T STAND IT

I want my dad and I want him now.
I feel like an out-of-control two-year-old and
my worry for him is tearing me apart.
What if someone hurts him before he can get home?
What if someone puts him back in one of those cages where
they keep the undocumented immigrants locked up
and he gets the virus, and no doctor, and—
I've got to get him NOW!
Get him out! Get him back!
No matter what it takes.

Money. They said he needs money,
and I know where to get some.
I know where Gramma keeps her emergency cash
and where Mom keeps the rent money, which
isn't due for another week yet.
I know everyone wants Dad to get here fast,
so someone needs to get him money right away!
All I need to do is go to McAllen.
I think it's only about four hours away.
I can probably find him through his cousin.
Get him home before Mama even gets back
in the morning.
And then *everything* will be better.
So I just have to be strong and brave and
go grab a bus to McAllen.

RUNNING AWAY TO MCALLEN

I fill my backpack with several bottles of water
and two masks and a jacket for me and one for him.
I add some crackers and oranges in case we get hungry.
And a piece of paper with the cousin's address,
which I get out of Gramma's address book.
And a flashlight, just in case.
And a blanket. I don't know why.
And the money.

Then I bike downtown to the Greyhound bus station
with a big lump in my throat—and butterflies in my stomach
from the sounds of the night, maybe, or
maybe the idea that I will be alone and still remember
all those stories of La Llorona grabbing children who
are out at night. Alone.
But I don't care what happens to me. I don't
care at all. The only thing that matters is Dad.

So even though I jump at every sound,
I hold on to my courage like it's a rope tossed to me
in a stormy ocean.
Until someone behind me grabs my shoulder and says,
Hey! Where are YOU going so late at night?

CRYING ON THE CURB

He was coming back from the gas station.
Had just sold the last of his mom's baked goodies
and was eager to get home for supper.
But now he's sitting on the curb with me,
and every tear and fear and frustration
is pouring out of me.

I HAVE to! Don't you understand?! I plead.

Celi! Don't YOU understand? Chato shouts,
more sure and strong than I'd ever heard him be.
*What will happen to your poor mom
if she gets home and you're not there?*

*And what if your dad gets home tomorrow,
all happy to be together, and his m'ijita preciosa
is LOST, or HURT, or KIDNAPPED!*

*And your poor papá—he'll feel like it's all
HIS fault! And wish he'd NEVER sent a message
that he was coming home!*

I'm already crying.
And THAT thought makes me cry some more.
He's a grown-up, Chato reminds me.
He's smart. He'll get here soon.
Yes, Chato is right.

Quiet, Gentle, Strong, Kind Chato is Absolutely
Right.

Suddenly, I gasp, *Gramma!*
Gramma's alone! I've got to get back!
Chato's stomach growls in agreement.
And I leave him my oranges and fly
back home on my bike.

SO HAPPY

Mama is so happy because Dad called her!
He said he'd be home after he finishes taking time
to quarantine. (I hadn't thought about that!)
And Gramma's feeling better and her doctor
says she just has allergies.
So Mama is singing and baking cookies nonstop.
She's so happy, she even suggests I invite
Liz, Cata, and Chato over to help eat them!
I smile as she chalks off spaces six feet apart
on our driveway, where we can sit and socially distance
while we munch on Mama's cookies.

It feels great to be happy again.

PRECIOUS GOLD

My friends are all together again!
Everyone's hair is longer—and now our smiles are bigger.
The smiles grow even wider when I tell them
my dad is finally, truly, on his way home.

Guess I blew it, I say after
Chato tells them what I almost did last night.

Híjole, Celi, when you blow it,
you do it BIG-TIME! says Cata.
Yeah, I know. I guess it WAS kind of impulsive . . .
But y'all don't understand what it's like
to be without your dad for almost a whole year . . .

Hey, Cata blurts out. *Who SAYS we don't understand!!!*
I don't have a mom OR dad! Anymore, anyway.
Thank goodness for my grandma's sister,
who adopted me when I was small.
My tía is WAY cool, so when folks say,
You don't have a DAD?!
I say, You don't have a GRANDMA'S SISTER?!
And the way Cata says this makes us all laugh.

Liz chimes in, in her wise, quiet way,
Everybody's family is different.
Some don't have a dad. Or a mom. Or a grandparent.

Some don't even have a best friend.
But look at us—we have three best friends!

Yeah, Cata agrees, *but we coulda lost you, Celi,*
and turned that THREE into just TWO!
She shakes her head and whistles low.
Still, I think you're amazingly brave to even TRY.

We're ALL brave, I say. *We survived these last few months.*

Most of us, Liz adds gently. *God bless Mr. Mason.*
We all nod and sit quietly as the sun begins to set.

I watch it cast its golden light onto the shining faces
of my friends, revealing them.
And I know they are
precious gold.

WE HUMANS ARE SELF-CENTERED

I call Chato to tell him the days are going too slow
as I wait for my dad to come home.
He says he'll swing by on his bike, and while I wait for him,
I realize I've never heard him talk about *his* father.
Just about his mom and four brothers.
And I realize I've never asked him.
I was too focused on my own problems.

So today, I ask gently, *You never talk about your father . . .*
And he answers with a sadness in his voice.

I haven't seen him since my youngest brother was born.
In a way, they're lucky—they hardly remember him—so
they don't miss him like I do.

You think he'll ever come back to see you?

I don't know. It's been so long now, over five years.
But it still hurts just as much. I guess
some scars go deep and still sting like fire.
Father's Day is coming, and it's always a tough holiday.

I know how hard some holidays can be, Chato. I'm sorry.

I'm sorry for you too.

The coolness of evening is in the air,
and we both seem to feel a little calmer.
Sometimes, even if a problem isn't solved
and isn't changed, when you're able to tell a friend,
it takes a little of the edge off your pain.

Then Mama comes out with a big caldera of soup
for him to take home to his family.
And when he leaves, with that big caldo pot balanced
in his little bike basket, he looks lighter and happier,
and I imagine
I do too.

JUNETEENTH

Today's Juneteenth, so I'm thinking about freedom.
Sometimes finding freedom seems like it takes forever.
For Indians, Mexicans, and so many groups . . .
And for Blacks, it's gone on *so* very long.
After President Lincoln declared enslaved people free,
lots of landowners kept the news a secret.
In Texas it wasn't till June 19, 1865,
two whole years after Lincoln's declaration,
that the people all got word
that they indeed were free.
So they first celebrated their freedom on that day
and called it Juneteenth, for short.

And still today, the struggle goes on.
More needs to be done—so everyone can vote,
attend good schools, work and live wherever they want,
without being stereotyped as criminals, or hurt.

Freedom isn't a *thing* you can stick in a *box*
and say, "There it is."
It's a living struggle we keep protecting every day,
each one of us a warrior, defending Freedom's way.

FATHER'S DAY

Father's Day is coming and there are a thousand things
I want to say as I try to write a poem about
my superhero, my papá, my wonderful dad,
who makes me feel safe and makes me feel glad
that I'm his kid and get to hear his jokes and dreams.

But I can't even think clearly enough to write.
All I can think of is that my dad is coming.
In days, he'll be here!

So instead of writing, I'm just gonna wait.
And imagine him here.
Strong and healthy,
smiling and tall.
Home.
Safe and embraced in our arms.
And that hug, I know,
will say it all.

HOME

It's a quiet moment
right after supper
but before anyone feels like clearing the table
or doing the dishes or turning on the TV.

For some reason we all look at each other at the same time.
Mom and Gramma and I.
In a moment that will stay engraved in our minds
forever.

Then a sound on the porch makes our breath stop.
Our eyes freeze.

He walks in the door, just like that.
Just like I've seen it in my head a thousand hungry-to-see-him times,
but better.

Dad is HOME
and the hunger
is all filled.

CATCHING LIGHTNING BUGS AT NIGHT

Dad and I have always loved lightning bugs.
Loved catching them gently in our cupped hands,
making a door with our thumbs
to watch them light up,
then making a wish before letting them go.

But tonight, catching them is not a dream,
not a memory.
Dad is really HOME.
It's really HIM. Right. Here.
All day I've felt his strong arms around me.
Hugging me as if he will never let go.

I jump up now and catch a lightning bug,
make a wish for everyone
to be free, and I let that beautiful glowing creature
fly high.

I ask Dad if he wants us to buy
chocolate ice cream or butter pecan
for our family picnic tomorrow. He says,
YOU pick, mi chula.
And I say, *No. YOU!*
And he says, *No. YOU!*
I want YOU to do what you want.
Do everything YOU want in life.
That's why we came here.

That's why I came here.
So you could be free
to do what YOU want.

And I know
he's not talking
about ice cream.

THE FIRST WHOLE DAY DAD'S HOME

The first whole day Dad's home
feels like all the celebrations of my life
rolled into one.
Mama is singing loud and happy,
dancing a cumbia in every room of the house.
Gramma is full of stories and jokes
and handing us every possible treat to eat.
Tía and Jade come over,
bringing supper and even cascarones!
And all of us are laughing and
beaming so hard, it feels like
my smile will permanently stretch my face.
Then, when Dad says, *How's my big girl been?*
I cuddle in close to tell him, and
Jade squeezes in between us
and I realize she needs his attention too,
so I set her on his lap, and we all hug.
And I realize
how much more I need to learn to notice
OTHERS' needs
and also, maybe,
how much I've grown.

CHATO WAS RIGHT

Chato was right
that my dad would
make it home on his own.

Dad IS smart and an adult.
And he did everything he could
the right way, the best he could.
And he was one of the lucky ones.
His papers were granted and
permission was given
for him to come home.

And he even quarantined himself
two weeks after being released
to make extra sure
he was healthy
and wouldn't infect
his *Mamá Tere,*
his *M'ijita Preciosa,*
and his *La Reina de Mi Corazón*
(that's what he calls Mom).

I hope I'll grow up
to be as smart and brave and kind
as you are, Papacito,
I whisper in his ear,

using the word I used for him
when I was little.

You will, M'ijita Preciosa,
you will be all that,
and even more.

RUNNING INTO SOMEONE WHO KNEW ME IN FIRST GRADE

Hey, aren't you Tere?
the boy says.
I knew you back in the old barrio,
back when you lived on San Fernando Street
and we used to all play baseball together
in the empty lot.
The big kids, the teenagers,
and us little preschoolers, you and me,
knocking around, pretending to hit the ball,
pretending to run for home base,
and the big kids pretending to let us get there.
And you used to talk a LOT when you were little.
Then you got real quiet later.
Remember that?

Yeah, I do, I say.
I remember.

Yeah.
I'm Tere.
Tere, and a Whole lot more.
A WHOLE
Lot More.

OUR OWN SECRET LANGUAGE

Gramma looks at me, and I can still see
the "Ay, que chula" honeyed messages in her eyes.
But there is something else there too.
Something new.
Something that says *I love you* in a new, proud way.
She looks straight at me and says,
Así es la vida. That's the way life is.
But she keeps her gaze right on me,
sending me those unspoken words we both still hear.
Like our own secret language,
our own Guerrera Changemaker Warrior language.

Yes, life tried to slap my mouth shut,
but whatever life throws at you,
you grab it and weave it into your song, celebrate it.
You change it and spice it to suit YOUR dreams,
whether they're dreams to write or dreams to sing
or dreams to build, or teach or heal or invent or
cross oceans or borders or walls of fear.
Whatever life throws at you, it feeds you.
It makes you stronger. It becomes
part of your shield.

THEY DON'T HAVE THE POWER

Sometimes
they try to take everything
away from you.
Sometimes
they actually do.
But then you look inside
and find something there
they can't even see
and they can't even
understand,
and so
they don't have the power
to see it,
touch it,
or take it away.

They don't have the power.
But You
Do.

You are all that has happened to you
and all that you dream to be
and all the possibilities,
whether reached or not.
And all of your story
and all of your name
and all you have loved

and all you choose to celebrate.
All of you, as warriors for the good,
Guerrera, Guerrero,
this knowledge, this courage,
this ALL inside you
will be
your shield
will be
your POWER.

AUTHOR'S NOTE

This novel in verse, while fictional, is based on the lives and experiences of many individuals in South Texas and throughout the nation. This story is told from the perspective of a twelve-year-old Chicana girl struggling to deal with the stresses of growing up in a turning point in history when anti-immigrant sentiments, deportations, racism, the caging of immigrant children, the killing of young Black people, the resistance to Black Lives Matter events, pandemic disease, and environmental crises challenge her struggle to reclaim her own identity, history, and power to make her own decisions about what she thinks and what she chooses to celebrate. She and her friends, through reading; questioning; writing letters, poems, and speeches; and planning actions to raise awareness, attempt to redefine themselves and change their world. This book is meant to create a discourse between readers and the people they value, as well as to be used as a learning tool to stimulate conversations about social justice, equality, cultural and linguistic biases, and the power of friendship.

ABOUT THE AUTHOR

One of the most anthologized Chicana writers, Dr. Carmen Tafolla has published many books for children and adults. She is the recipient of numerous awards, including two Américas Awards, seven International Latino Book Awards, two Tomás Rivera Book Awards, two ALA Notable Books, and the Art of Peace Award. She was the first Latina to be awarded the prestigious Charlotte Zolotow Award (for her picture book *What Can You Do with a Paleta?* illustrated by Magaly Morales). A native of the west side barrios of San Antonio, Dr. Tafolla is a Professor Emeritus at the University of Texas at San Antonio. She is the former Poet Laureate of the state of Texas, and prior to that served as the first Poet Laureate of San Antonio. She is currently at work on the full adult biography of Emma Tenayuca, and on an accompanying chapter book. Listen to Carmen Tafolla's interview and poetry reading, "Empowering Mexican-American Youth Through Writing," with Maria Hinojosa on NPR Latino USA.

LAND ACKNOWLEDGMENT

The city where this story takes place and where it was written is the traditional homeland of many Indigenous nations, including the Tap Pilam Coahuiltecan peoples, the Payayas, Sanas, Tamiques, Pampopas, Carrizos/Comecrudos, Aranamas, and others. Many of these peoples were later declared by law of the Republic of Texas in 1837 to be considered and treated as "part of the Mexican people," thereby legally distancing them from their rights and standing as native residents of this land.

We gratefully acknowledge the role that ancestral nations have had in creating this settlement of peoples along the Yanaguana River and the respect for life and harmony that they have left to their many descendants who live and work in the San Antonio area today. Many have benefited from the special, respectful spirit of this place and the values it has taught us.